FORGOTTEN
CRIMES

A gripping psychological suspense thriller

ANNA WILLETT

THE
BOOK
FOLKS

Paperback edition published by

The Book Folks

London, 2018

ISBN 978-1-9867-5300-5

www.thebookfolks.com

This book includes BACKWOODS MEDICINE, a bonus five-chapter prequel to Anna Willett's first thriller, BACKWOODS RIPPER.

Chapter One

Gloria Kline cursed under her breath and turned her car into the Easy Eight parking lot. The flat slab of bitumen reserved for the bar's clientele looked white, bleached by decades of relentless sun. In some areas, black streaks marred the surface with trails of rubber left by late night burnouts. In her dreams, the bar always rose out of a pond of mist like a sinister grey monster. But in the harsh afternoon sun, it looked like a grimy washed-out watering hole about five years late for its appointment with a wrecking ball. *I must be crazy to be back here*, Gloria thought with a shudder of disgust.

She pulled up under a dented "customers only" sign and turned the engine off. Certain that no one would bother checking if she was a customer or not, she climbed out and clicked the lock button on her keys. Honey's Café was only a short walk from the bar. If Fryer Street hadn't been overflowing with lunchtime traffic, she wouldn't have come within a mile of the bar, let alone park near it. *It's only a run-down bar*, she reminded herself, *nothing here can hurt me… Not anymore.*

Gloria picked her way across the cracked and pot-hole dimpled lot, a difficult task in high-heeled, strappy sandals. When she reached the corner of Fryer Street, she hesitated. She hadn't intended to look back but a shivery sensation caressed the nape of her neck. The feeling that she was being watched made her glance over her shoulder.

The building's white-washed walls had faded to a dirty grey and the large half-dome-shaped windows looked like they'd been painted black. *Probably to help the drunks convince themselves they're not starting too early.* The place had always been a bit of a dive, but now it looked derelict. She wrinkled her nose and not for the first time wondered why Rhetty had chosen this part of town for their lunch over all the more ritzy establishments closer to home.

She forced the bar out of her mind and headed for the corner. Fryer Street, mostly lined with utes and minivans, practically danced with activity; a world away from the stark concrete slab surrounding the Easy Eight. Tradies in steel-capped boots and hi-vis vests trekked in and out of fast food establishments clutching greasy brown paper bags and large bottles of soft drink. She heard car doors slamming and plastic awnings flapping: a welcome relief from the silence of the Easy Eight parking lot. *It couldn't have been that quiet, not this close to so much activity*, Gloria puzzled.

She noticed a cluster of plastic chairs on the footpath outside Honey's. An elderly man wearing a flat cap, and sipping from a red mug, occupied the chair nearest the entrance. He had the yellow, heavily-lined skin of a long-term smoker. *An alfresco area*, Gloria thought grimly and slowed her pace.

A metre or so away from the chairs, a woman stood motionless, her back to the street as though she were watching something inside the café. The bones of her shoulders jutted up, poking through her loose-fitting white T-shirt. Over one skinny shoulder hung a huge, ugly, denim bag. Gloria almost looked away, dismissing the woman as a local cleaner or shop worker, but something about the way she stood, the angle of her neck, seemed familiar. The woman turned and looked in Gloria's direction. A smile lifted the corners of her taunt mouth.

Gloria almost turned to see who the woman was smiling at when it hit her. *Rhetty*. Her always plump, but bubbly, friend was now a gaunt, defeated-looking woman standing in the doorway of a shabby café. But more than just the weight loss, something about the way Rhetty looked didn't feel right. Usually glamorous and stylish, today she was dressed in grey cargo pants and a cheap white T-shirt. Her shoulder-length blonde hair was twisted into a tight bun at the back of her head. The overall effect was sad and dowdy, two words that she'd never associated with Rhetty before.

Gloria's pace faltered. Her mind ran in a dozen different directions. How had this happened? What had caused such a dramatic change? She forced a smile and approached her friend.

"Sorry I'm late, I had to park around the corner at the Easy Eight. What a dive." Gloria bent slightly and kissed Rhetty on the cheek.

"No, that's fine. I just got here. Um…Speaking of the Easy Eight, would you mind if we went there instead? I need a drink," Rhetty said, her eyes darting everywhere but at Gloria.

Gloria nearly laughed, but noticed Rhetty's pinched mouth and knotted brow.

"Okay, yeah. A drink would be great," Gloria's tone rang out a notch too cheerful. The man in the flat cap gave Gloria a startled look before returning to his drink.

The two women turned and headed back towards the corner. Gloria squinted against the harsh afternoon sun and wished she'd remembered her sunglasses. A soft-drink truck rattled past them and a gust of hot air blew up from the pavement. Gloria grimaced and slipped her hand into the crook of Rhetty's elbow drawing her friend closer. They'd been walking this way since they were in primary school. It was one of those things best friends did without even thinking, but this time, Gloria was struck by how fragile Rhetty felt – hollow, like a small bird.

The two walked in silence.

"Rhetty, you're really scaring me." She pulled her friend to a stop outside a bookie's place. The TV blared out the latest horse race. Behind them a man swore and stepped around the girls, clipping Rhetty's shoulder – he strode past without apology. The door to the betting shop slammed open. Gloria jumped and squeezed Rhetty's forearm. The corner lay just ahead, once they turned it, they'd be back at the bar.

"What's going on? You don't drink in the middle of the day and you look like…" *A bag of bones*. "Like you've lost ten kilos. Are you sick? Is that what it is?" Gloria tried to keep her voice even. She let go of Rhetty's arm and touched the side of her forehead where the beginnings of a headache burned its way across her temple.

"No, I'm not sick," Rhetty said quietly. "But I need to talk to you. Not yet though, I really do need a drink first."

She took Gloria's arm and pulled her towards the corner.

Gloria didn't resist, but her mind spun with questions and fears. If Rhetty wasn't sick, what could be making her behave this way? Her fiancé, Malcolm? Were they having problems? If they were, Gloria had no doubt Malcolm would be the cause.

The mid-afternoon sun scorched the parking lot, softening the ancient bitumen and forcing Gloria to walk on her toes so her heels didn't stick. Beads of sweat popped out on the back of her neck and clung to her hair. She glanced at Rhetty who seemed oblivious to the heat; head up, her eyes remained fixed on the dark wood door of the bar.

"I hate this place," Gloria muttered as they neared the entrance.

"What?" Rhetty asked.

"Nothing. I just… I just don't like this bar. It's a dive," Gloria said and gave a weak laugh.

"You used to love this place." Rhetty sounded concerned.

Gloria clenched her teeth with such force that her gums ached. Everything about the Easy Eight reminded her of a time she'd rather forget. Standing in the shadow of the building, time reversed itself and brought her back to when everything went wrong.

But this wasn't about her. She squared her shoulders and gripped the tarnished brass door handle, pushing forward with a false air of casualness.

The first thing that struck Gloria was the smell. The smell *and* the dimness. The air was heavy with the stench of stale beer and fried food; the combination brought bile to her throat, thick and sour. A taste that couldn't be scrubbed away. The low lights did little to disguise the threadbare carpet, and the cracked and scarred dark wooden bar.

She felt Rhetty enter and moved aside so they both stood in the doorway. Gloria glanced over her shoulder and watched the heavy door swing shut. *Entombed.* She shuddered at the thought.

"I'll find us a seat," Rhetty said, and moved past Gloria towards the row of booths to the right of the bar.

"Wait," Gloria breathed, not sure why she whispered in the almost empty bar. "What do you want to drink?"

Rhetty turned and for a moment, a smile played around her mouth, but the look vanished. "Whiskey with ice. Have you forgotten?" There was an undercurrent to her voice that Gloria couldn't quite place.

Rhetty turned and walked to the last booth nearest the toilets and sat with her back to the bar. Gloria's eyes flickered to the toilet door and the tarnished gold sign *Gals.* It made the seedy toilet sound like a happy meeting place for young women. She blinked hard, then turned away and stepped up to the bar.

A man in a blue and white checked shirt, baggy shorts, and thongs sat on a stool nursing a beer. Gloria couldn't help noticing his feet were dirty, as though he'd been walking through mud. She pulled her gaze away and scanned the area behind the bar, hoping to order their drinks and get out of the place as swiftly as possible. Three lone drinkers dotted the left side of the bar; all men.

"Back again? What can I get you?"

The question came from the man with the dirty feet. For a second Gloria thought she misheard him.

"Sorry, what did you say?" She prayed he wasn't trying to pick her up.

"What do you want to drink?" He said the words slowly as though he were talking to a child.

"I… Are you the –"

"Yes. I'm the barman. I'm just taking a break, but I'm happy to interrupt my special time for a lovely lady like you." He swivelled around on the stool and openly surveyed her body from head to toe.

Gloria felt herself flush, suddenly very aware that in a short silk sundress and heels, she was overdressed for a place like the Easy Eight Bar. And, that Rhetty and her were the only women in the place.

"A white wine and a whiskey with ice," she said, tilting her head up, trying to sound confident.

The barman smiled with yellowed teeth, probably from a lifetime of heavy smoking. He stood and sauntered around the bar while she busied herself getting her purse out of her handbag. She glanced over at the booth where Rhetty sat, wanting to see if her friend watched, but Rhetty remained with her back to the bar.

After what felt like an eternity, the barman set the drinks in front of her. She paid him, picked up the glasses, and opened her mouth to thank him when he leaned forward and gave her a knowing wink. "Don't drink 'em all at once."

Does he recognise me? Does he remember that night? Heart pounding, she turned away and almost stumbled. Some of the wine sloshed onto her hand.

"Uh, oh, looks like you've already had a few," the barman called as she walked away on shaky legs.

Gloria put the drinks down and slipped into the booth.

"Thanks," Rhetty mumbled and picked up the whiskey. Gloria watched, mouth agape, as she downed it in one go and slammed the glass back onto the table.

"God, you weren't kidding when you said you needed a drink."

Rhetty ignored the comment and held Gloria's gaze.

"Joanna's back."

Chapter Two

March 5th 2011

Joanna, a towering figure in black with dark spiky hair and eyes that could devour you whole, stood in the doorway of the Easy Eight Bar surveying the crowd. A herd of bodies swallowed the bar; Eighties pop music blasted from the jukebox and the scent of draft beer and perfume filled the air. She checked her watch: 9:15. She was late.

Spotting a group of three men near the bar, Joanna made her way towards them. As she approached, a man in his thirties with bulging biceps and dirty blonde hair, turned towards her. His eyes appraised her before he nudged his friend who also turned and gave her the once over.

"Hi. Are you looking for me," the blonde asked with a cheeky smile that didn't quite reach his eyes. His dark-haired friend sniggered.

"Maybe." Joanna looked him up and down.

"What do you –"

"Joanna! I thought you'd stood me up." Rhetty grabbed her arm and pulled her away from the men. She tried to look annoyed, but couldn't hide her smile.

Joanna leaned down and kissed her friend's cheek. Her silky soft skin and hair smelling of apples toyed with Joanna's senses. She let her cheek linger against Rhetty's for a second enjoying the sensation.

"Sorry, babe. My roommate was supposed to give me a lift but as usual, she kept me waiting."

"That's fine, I'm just teasing," Rhetty laughed, and waved her hand dismissively. "Come on, Gloria's waiting." She pushed her way through the densely-packed bodies.

"Hang on, I wanna get a drink first."

"No need. I already got you one."

Joanna forced a smile, Rhetty had a way of manoeuvring people that was amusing and irritating at the same time. Tonight, the former outweighed the latter. Joanna nodded that she was following, but couldn't resist a backward glance at the blonde. He gave her a slow wink and turned away. Joanna suppressed a satisfied grin and followed Rhetty as she sashayed her round hips towards the booth at the end of the bar. Her appeal was undeniable, *and* she had deep pockets, but sometimes Joanna felt like the woman smothered her.

And then there was *Gloria*. Wherever Rhetty went, Gloria was never far behind, craving attention and approval. It seemed an invisible string bound them together, and no matter how hard she pulled, Joanna couldn't find a way to snap the cord. *Maybe I'm not pulling hard enough*, Joanna thought.

Gloria sat with her back to the wall, head slightly tilted up. She looked supremely confident and soap opera pretty.

Joanna noticed that her eyes were trained on Rhetty as the two of them approached the table.

"I found her," Rhetty sang and slipped into the booth opposite Gloria.

"Hi," Joanna said, and sat next to Rhetty.

"Who were those guys at the bar?" Gloria asked, sipping her rum and Coke.

Joanna held Gloria's gaze and gave her standard 'what does it matter to you' shrug. Gloria's eyes narrowed for a second before turning to Rhetty and softening.

"What's the plan for tonight?" Joanna asked.

"We're–"

"Rhetty and I have a little tradition," Gloria interrupted. "We celebrate the beginning of autumn with a girls' night."

"It's silly I know, but we–"

"Don't apologise for the things we do," Gloria snapped, cutting Rhetty off. "Just because she doesn't understand doesn't make it silly." She paused, licked her lips and turned her blue eyes back to Joanna. "What I mean is, things make sense to us because we've been friends for so long."

Gloria clearly resented her presence. *Time to show her just how much Rhetty wants me*, Joanna thought and started to rise.

"Look, I don't want to crash your tradition. We can get together another night."

"Don't you dare leave," Rhetty cried and grabbed Joanna's arm.

Pleased with Rhetty's reaction, Joanna smiled at Gloria's sour expression as she sat back down. "Tell me more about this tradition."

Gloria shrugged and looked away while Rhetty explained, "Every autumn, usually the first week—" She pushed a strand of hair behind her ear and licked her lips. "We, that is Gloria and I, get together and spend the night partying."

"Sounds like a normal Saturday night to me," Joanna said.

"It's nothing like your sloppy weekends," Gloria snapped. Her upper lip twitched as if she was trying to keep it from curling in disgust. Joanna watched the woman's perfectly glossed mouth straining to remain neutral. A small jet of anger flared in her stomach.

"Come on, Gloria," Rhetty cooed. "We've gotten pretty sloppy on more than one occasion." When Gloria didn't respond, Rhetty continued. "Partying is probably the wrong word, but we do drink and dance. Usually here." She flapped her hand palm up at the crowd. "But the main part. The bit that always stays the same is finishing off the night at Gloria's holiday house. We've done that every autumn for seven years."

"What's the significance of autumn?" Joanna looked from one woman to the other, enjoying the way Gloria's pretty mouth was now drawn down in a tight line.

Rhetty paused and glanced at Gloria. *For what*, Joanna wondered. *Approval?*

"Our parents died in the summer," Gloria said flatly.

"Not all during the same summer," Rhetty added. "But nevertheless, summer's…" Her voice wavered. "Summer's better when it's over." She stretched her arm across the table and Gloria took her hand. *All we need now,* Joanna thought, *is for Bette Midler to start singing.*

"Well here's to a new season," Joanna said, raising her glass.

Rhetty let go of Gloria's hand and picked up her glass. "To a new season," the three women said, and clicked glasses.

"And a wild night," Joanna added.

Chapter Three

March 4th 2015

"What do you mean Joanna's back? How can she be back?" Gloria sputtered, still shaking her head.

Rhetty looked around before she spoke, as though there might be someone listening.

"Calm down Gloria. Drink your wine," she ordered in a calm voice.

"I don't want my wine, Rhetty. I want you to stop acting crazy and explain to me what's going on." Gloria pushed the glass away from her and grabbed her bag. "I've got to get out of here."

"Stop it!"

The anger in Rhetty's voice surprised her. She dropped her bag onto the cracked blue vinyl seat and looked down at her lap. When she looked up Rhetty was staring at her waiting for her to calm down.

"Rhetty," Gloria said in a steady voice. "What is going on?"

Rhetty's face, clear of make-up, looked drawn and pale. Her blue eyes reflected the weight of a terrible burden. Gloria wanted to look away, change the subject, run from the bar and never come back; but she didn't move. Instead she waited for her friend to speak.

"It *is* Joanna, she's back." There was a flat certainty in the way Rhetty spoke that made Gloria's stomach drop.

"She can't be back. You know that's impossible."

"I *saw* her," Rhetty whispered. "It was her, I know it."

Gloria leaned back in her seat and let out a long breath. Joanna had been out of their lives for a long time, but her shadow hung over them like a spectre. Its presence had changed their friendship. Changed *them*. The last thing Gloria wanted was to be reminded of things she'd fought so hard to forget. And now here she sat, back in the one place she'd promised herself she'd never return to. She clenched her fists under the table and glared at Rhetty.

"Hey, I know we're not as close as we used to be, but why are you doing this? Why did you bring me here? It's like you're *trying* to be cruel." Gloria held her breath, willing Rhetty to tell her it was all a silly game or a mistake. Instead Rhetty remained unmoved.

"I know it's difficult for you to get your head around, but I know what I saw and," she paused, then said in little more than a whisper, "I spoke to her."

A sudden sound pierced the air. Gloria jumped forward in her seat. Her ribs collided with the table and set off a dull ache in her side. She looked around and noticed the barman with the dirty feet had disappeared. *Probably gone around the other side of the bar to investigate the noise.*

Gloria put her right hand on her side and tried to massage the spot she'd whacked against the table.

"Are you okay?" Rhetty asked.

"No. No, I'm not okay," Gloria said, wincing. "I think I've cracked a fucking rib." She grabbed the wine glass with her left hand and took a large swig. "Okay, if we're going to do this, you'd better tell me everything." She took another sip and put the glass down. "Come on, let's hear it."

Rhetty let out a huge breath and nodded. "It started about six weeks ago. I drove home after my workout, Malcolm was away." She gave a 'what's new' shrug and continued. "I went into the bathroom to take a shower and I *felt* something." She scratched the side of her neck and grimaced. "I know it sounds like something out of a horror movie, but the air changed and –"

"The air changed?" Gloria repeated. "Seriously, *Rhetty!*"

"I know, I know." She held up her hand like a crossing guard. "Just let me finish before you start telling me I'm crazy. Let me get it all out and then you can decide for yourself."

Gloria sat back with a frown and held her side. She nodded for Rhetty to continue.

"The air in the bathroom changed, like all the heat had been sucked out and replaced with cold air. My first thought was the air conditioner, but I knew I hadn't turned it on, and even if that was it, the bathroom door was closed and the closest vent's in the bedroom. There's no way it could change the air temperature inside the bathroom like that.

"I tried to open the bathroom door, but the handle wouldn't turn. I don't mean it wouldn't open, the door handle wouldn't move; it felt cemented in place and made of ice." She wrapped her arms around herself as if she were reliving the moment and could feel the cold on her skin. "I tried to stay calm, but I could feel myself panicking. Then…Then I smelled *Voyage*. It's what Joanna used to wear –"

"I know what it is." Gloria swallowed back the urge to say more, and let her friend continue.

"Well, then I *really* panicked. I started pounding on the door. I was just about to climb out the window when the handle finally turned and I burst out of the bathroom." She let out a long shuddering breath. "It took me two hours to work up the courage to go back in there. By then, everything seemed normal." She gave a wry laugh. "I convinced myself that nothing had really happened and maybe I'd had a panic attack or something."

"Maybe you did have one. Maybe because Malcolm's always going away, you got spooked. It happens." Gloria didn't like where the story was heading.

"Yes. That's what I convinced myself of, but then other things happened. About a week later I drove home after a late meeting with a client; she had a custody hearing coming up and needed a bit of hand-holding. I'd nearly reached the house, had just driven past the golf course… you know that part of the road where it's mostly bush and not much light?"

Gloria nodded.

"Anyway, I saw her in the road. Not in the middle, just off the curb. She had her back to me, sort of strolling along. Just like that night when we picked her up. Everything was the same. She wore the same clothes: black pants and a black cut-off shirt. And the radio… It was playing –"

"Say My Name," Gloria whispered.

Rhetty's eyes widened with surprise. "You remember?"

"Of course I remember. But Rhetty, what you're saying is impossible. Joanna is dead. She's been dead for four years."

Chapter Four

Gloria watched as Rhetty manoeuvred her way out of the bar holding her phone to her ear. She turned sideways to get through the crowd of bodies in what was likely an over-capacity night. Gloria glanced at her watch: 9:50 pm.

"What have you got for me?" Gloria asked Joanna, keeping one eye on the door as it swung shut behind Rhetty.

Joanna eyed her for a moment. "How much have you had to drink?"

Gloria knew Joanna couldn't care less about her or what sort of state she got herself into. She wondered about the false concern.

"Rhetty's not here, Joanna. You can drop the kind-hearted routine," Gloria said and took her purse out of her clutch bag. "Just give me the stuff."

Joanna shrugged and pulled down the front of her top revealing a black lacy bra. She glanced over her shoulder before reaching into the padded cup and producing a small piece of foil.

"Here," she said and slid her hand under the table.

Gloria took the package.

"How much?"

"Eighty."

"What? Why so much?" Gloria leaned forward.

"Price has gone up. Anyway, what do you care? You're loaded. You can afford it." Joanna nodded towards Gloria's bag. "How much did that cost? Three, four hundred?" Her voice was thick with resentment.

"That's not the point. I don't like being ripped off," Gloria said defensively.

Joanna loved making her feel small, as if having money was something to be ashamed of. She noticed the look of smug satisfaction on Joanna's face and wished she could take the words back.

Gloria took the money out and slipped it under the table. She felt Joanna's fingers grip the notes and then her wrist. Gloria tried to pull back, but Joanna held her with surprising strength.

"Let go," Gloria hissed.

"Be careful with those tablets, they'll send you down the rabbit hole and into wonderland." Joanna's voice was mocking, heavy with menace. "You might never come back."

Gloria twisted her wrist and managed to pull her hand free.

"Fuck you!" she choked out, hating the whiny sound of her voice. She opened the foil and popped the two tablets, washing them down with the last of her rum and Coke.

Joanna laughed and clapped her hands. "Get ready, the fun's about to start."

"It sounds like you two are getting along," Rhetty said and put her hand on Joanna's shoulder.

"How's Malcolm?" Joanna asked still smiling at Gloria.

Rhetty shrugged. "Don't worry about him. Who wants another drink?"

"Joanna just offered to get them," Gloria said.

Joanna nodded at Gloria and stood.

"What would you like, babe?" Joanna asked leaning her arms on Rhetty's shoulders. Even in heels Rhetty's head barely reached Joanna's collar bone.

"Just a Coke. Remember, I'm driving tonight," Rhetty said, smiling up at her.

Gloria watched the exchange with a growing sense of resentment. She'd known Rhetty since they were children, but since Joanna became a part of their lives, she felt their closeness slipping away. *Is this what a parent feels like when their child grows up and realises they can get along without them? Maybe Rhetty doesn't need me anymore?*

Gloria looked around the room so she wouldn't have to look into Rhetty's eyes. When Gloria's mother died, Rhetty had told her that they would always have each other; they would be each other's family, and whatever happened they would take care of one another.

Gloria felt her eyes moisten. Rhetty's words had been the rope she'd clung to when times were tough or grief threatened to overtake her. Now she'd become a third wheel. One of those annoying needy friends that didn't know when to give up.

"Are you okay? You look a bit pale." Rhetty's voice sounded like an echo over the thudding of the music, or was the thudding coming from Gloria's heart?

"I'm going to dance," she muttered.

Gloria stood up and stumbled out of the booth. Her heart beat in time with the music and her limbs tingled with energy. She wanted to shrug off her old self and all the pathetic hurt she felt. She hoped the pills would hurry up and do their thing – she didn't want to remember anymore. She pushed through the crowd following the music.

A good-sized group danced around the jukebox where the lights were dimmed. A lone blue strobe skimmed the area. She moved forward and made her way into the tangle of limbs and bodies. Tilting her head up, she swayed and thrust to the music. She couldn't quite place the song, but it didn't matter, all she needed was the thumping; the highs and lows to carry her away.

The heat and tension ebbed from her body, replaced by a soaring sense that anything might be possible. Faces came in and out of focus. With each turn she became aware of a figure standing within arm's length of the writhing bodies. At first, only his silhouette showed – dark and solid amongst blurred heads and arms. Then his face, familiar, but unknown came into focus. Gloria squinted, watching him shrink into blackness and then pop back to life.

He touched her arm and she shuddered, unsure if she'd moved towards him or he'd approached her. His blonde hair glistened under the blue lights that swept the dance floor. He whispered in her ear. The words were lost to the music, but his breath was hot. It bathed her skin in a tantalizing moistness and sent spirals of heat down her neck. She traced his arms with her fingertips and felt the swell of his muscles.

Then his mouth found hers; she pressed her body against his. He clung to her as though he would die if he released her. She could feel his heart beating against her chest, or was it her own heart trying to burst out of her body and melt into his?

Her back jerked and a gap opened between them. Gloria felt someone tugging her, pulling her away from him. She struggled, desperate to fall back into the warmth of his body.

"What are you doing?" The voice seemed familiar, but altered as though the words were being shouted down a tunnel.

Gloria turned, wanting to slap the sound away. Rhetty's face was white and stark; her mouth an angry line.

"Leave me alone," Gloria hissed baring her teeth and leaning closer to Rhetty's upturned face.

Her friend's mouth went from angry to surprised. The way her expression changed under the flickering lights was like watching a puppet show. Gloria couldn't contain the laughter. Rhetty pulled back and let go of her shirt. Now her mouth turned down. Gloria let another giggle escape as her hands searched for the body, the muscles, and that needy mouth.

"I'm going outside with Joanna. When I come back we're leaving," Rhetty's voice sounded like a trumpet. Gloria nodded and covered her mouth to stifle another fit of laughter.

She looked over Rhetty's shoulder to where Joanna stood near the main door shaking her head. The pitying look on her face took Gloria by surprise. She shook off grasping hands. She wanted to run at the woman and drag her finger nails across her supercilious face. Instead she stood motionless, watching the two women leave the bar.

A hand closed over her shoulder and turned her around. The floor shifted under Gloria's feet. She stumbled. An arm slid around her waist and once more she was enveloped.

"You okay, love?" His voice was velvet against her raw nerves.

She pulled him close and kissed him. His lips parted and she felt his tongue flick hers. A bolt of pleasure exploded in her stomach. She pushed her body against his, flattening her breasts against him.

"Come on." He pulled away from her then took her hand, leading her around the bar. Gloria didn't know how it was possible, but the crowd had swelled to twice its size. The bodies vibrated wall to wall.

Muscle-man pushed his way through the throng without a backward glance. Gloria stumbled forward in his wake. Even if she'd wanted to resist, she knew she couldn't free herself from his vice-like grip. *Where are we going?*

They reached the end booth. Gloria noticed a group of girls crowded around the table, clutching glasses and leaning forward in animated conversation. *Where's Rhetty?* Her thoughts felt foggy, fleeting, but she felt sure her friend was coming back for her. *Rhetty wouldn't leave me, would she?*

Her hand throbbed. She called to him to let go, but couldn't get the words past her numb lips. The tables disappeared as they reached the door to the ladies' room.

He turned and pulled her closer. Gloria struggled to keep both feet on the floor. Then, realising he was lifting her, she let herself go.

For an instant, she hung in the air. She felt light, weightless enough to take flight. She let out a joyful whoop and looked to her right catching a flash of the group of girls. They were laughing and nodding. Then they spun out of view and she came to rest inside the ladies' room.

The bright lights in the bathroom dazzled. Orange spots danced in front of her eyes. Strong hands raced up and down her sides, guiding her towards the sinks. She turned her head to the side and registered a girl moving away towards the door. Something about the startled look on the girl's face struck her as funny; another fit of giggles bubbled up and out of her mouth.

Her back hit the sink and a spike of pain seared up her spine. His mouth found hers again, muffling her gasp of shock. She pulled away and looked into his eyes. They looked grey under the florescent lights.

"What's your name?" she whispered.

"Call me Smiley."

The velvety tone had disappeared, his voice now harsh – dangerous. He put his hands on her waist and spun her around until she faced the mirror over the sink. In its reflection she saw herself; head tilted to the left, eyes hooded and mouth slightly open. He engulfed the space behind her, his size almost filling the mirror. His dirty blonde hair stood up in ragged spikes, his mouth now set in a determined line.

A tiny sliver of uncertainty crept into Gloria's thoughts. *What am I doing? What am I about to do?* Then his hands moved to her stomach and touched the bare flesh between her skirt and top and she shivered with delight. The skin on his fingers brushed rough against her flesh making her tremble. She watched his hands in the mirror as they travelled up, pushing up the thin fabric of her gold top until her breasts were exposed.

She groaned with pleasure and leaned back against him raising her arms behind her and hooking them around his neck. He kept his eyes on her in the mirror as he caressed and fondled her breasts. The room faded away until all she could see were their images in front of her.

His hands moved to her back and slid up to her neck. She allowed him to push her forward. She let go of his neck and braced herself on the sink, still watching him in the mirror. His face an unreadable mask, he pushed up her mini skirt and yanked at her underwear, which fell to her ankles.

Her breath came in urgent gasps as he pushed himself into her. She let out a moan of pleasure and jerked back onto him. Every nerve in her body pulsed in a magic wave. A sensation like nothing she'd ever experienced. She wanted to laugh and cry. She closed her eyes and the world behind her eyelids washed blue.

When she opened them something had changed. For a fraction of a second, she thought she was seeing double. The man behind her seemed to split into two, then she realised there was someone else in the room. He was shorter and had dark hair plastered to his head with grease. The overhead lights cast dark shadows around his eyes and cheeks giving him a hollow ghoulish appearance. The corners of his mouth turned up in what looked more like a sneer than a smile.

Gloria tried to stand and pull her top down but was pushed forward –her face shoved into the basin. The cold surface of the sink felt like ice against her cheek as her mouth and nose smashed against the drain. The smell of cleaning products and mould made her gag.

She struggled to turn away.

The hand clamped on the back of her neck squeezed and pressed her down harder. She heard laughter and felt another set of hands on her body.

"My turn."

The words cut through every other sensation. Gloria bucked like a wild animal desperate to break free. Her head hit the underside of the tap, pain sliced through her scalp. She tried to reach behind her to tear at the hand that held her neck, but his grip was unmovable.

The heightened pleasure she'd felt only moments ago was now replaced by terror and panic. Reality crashed through whatever poison Joanna had given her. She knew what was about to happen to her, but was powerless to stop it.

With sobriety came an exhaustion she'd never felt before. Her legs buckled and her breathing became laboured. She heard laughter behind her. Close and harsh. In the distance, with the opening and closing of the bathroom door, female laughter tinkled in as pop music pulsed.

Chapter Five

March 4th 2015

Gloria let out a heavy sigh and looked around the bar. The things Rhetty said made no sense. A nervous breakdown seemed the only rational explanation. God knows, Gloria had struggled with her own sanity many times since that night.

"Look," she said softly. "I know what this is."

"Do you?" Rhetty snapped.

Gloria could see the uncertainty in her friend's eyes and she felt a wave of sympathy towards her. *I wonder how long this has been going on? The easy answer: four years.*

That's when their lives changed. That's when everything had been turned upside down. And, as always, it came back to Joanna. *She* had caused this. She was the one who'd inserted herself into their lives and wreaked havoc.

"I know it's hard, but you can't let what happened ruin your life. Whatever you think you're seeing, it's just your mind." Gloria searched for the right words. "Like flashbacks." She reached across the table to touch Rhetty's hand.

Rhetty flinched and pulled away. Gloria couldn't help feeling hurt by the reaction. *Has our friendship really come to this?* Gloria put her hand back in her lap and tried to not look as wounded as she felt.

"It's not my mind, and it's not flashbacks. Something *is* happening. No … That's not right. Joanna is making this happen and we've got to do something before it's too late."

Gloria wanted to answer, but the barman returned carrying a dustpan and brush. She watched him over Rhetty's shoulder as he dumped it on the bar and muttered under his breath. He glanced over at her and caught her watching him. She looked back down at her lap before she could see his reaction.

"I think we should go to the police." Rhetty whispered out the words.

Gloria's attention snapped back. Rhetty's expression frightened her. A sort of blank determination that she suspected people had just before they jumped off multi-storey buildings.

"No. We agreed. We shouldn't even be talking about this." She tried to keep the desperation from her voice. "I want to help you, Rhetty. I really do, but you can't talk about going to the police."

"Then say you believe me."

"I … I'm trying to understand. It's just what you're talking about – well … it's not possible." Gloria bit her bottom lip. She waited for her to answer, but instead Rhetty rummaged through her bag.

It looked more like a denim sack than a handbag – oversized and shapeless. Nothing like the stylish little bags Rhetty used to carry. Gloria watched her friend; she frowned and shook her head. She noticed the neckline of Rhetty's T-shirt, yellowed with age and a small hole on the right sleeve. *I wonder if she slept in it?*

Rhetty pulled something out of her voluminous tote and put it on the table. For a second, Gloria thought she meant to show her something on her phone. She leaned closer and then stiffened. She stared at an outdated iPhone 3. The screen was broken, and the rubber case shredded.

"What's that?" Gloria grimaced.

Rhetty turned the phone over revealing the design on the back of the case: a cartoonish face with double slits for the eyes and a semi-circle mouth with a protruding tongue. The effect was a face squinting with laughter. Thick dirt caked its edges.

Gloria's stomach sank, and her mouth went dry. She stared at the phone. "Where did you get that?"

"It's hers," Rhetty whispered.

"I know." Gloria dragged her eyes away from the phone and fixed her gaze on Rhetty's. "What I want to know is *where* did you get it?"

Rhetty reached out and touched the phone, tracing her index finger over the face. Gloria shuddered. She wondered how the other woman could bare to touch it. Without thinking, she rubbed her palm on the front of her dress.

"I was doing some gardening," she paused, her finger still on the phone case. "I like gardening, it's relaxing, but I guess you didn't know that about me?" Rhetty said with a shrug.

Gloria noticed the accusatory edge to her tone, but was too focused on the phone to be stung by her words.

"Anyway," Rhetty continued. "I was planting some Chinese cabbage seedlings – autumn's a good time for planting," she said in a faraway voice and paused. "I hit something with my trowel." She frowned and picked up the broken phone. "I thought I'd hit a rock so I carried on digging, and then I uncovered this." She bent her wrist forwards as if she were offering the phone to Gloria.

"Please, put it away." Gloria held her hand up to ward the thing away.

She was sure she could smell the wet, earthy odour of dirt. The thought of touching it made her stomach churn. She turned her head away and swallowed the urge to vomit. When she looked back, the phone had vanished, presumably into Rhetty's cavernous handbag.

"Sorry." Rhetty's voice was soft, almost breathless. "But I had to show you. I had to make you *understand*."

"Understand what?" Gloria asked, trying to keep her voice even.

"That this is real. And … and I need your help." Rhetty let out a long breath, shutting her eyes. She looked like the weight of the world rested on her shoulders.

Gloria watched her friend. Her eyelids looked thin, almost transparent and colourless but for the blue veins that snaked across the pale skin...

* * *

They were both nine years old when they met. Gloria and her parents had just moved to Perth and it was her first day in Saint Catherine's School for Girls. Being the *new girl* was excruciating, but as always, Gloria held up her head and put on a brave face.

The hardest part of the day came with recess. Gloria followed her new classmates out onto a rolling lawn where they sat in little groups under the shade of ancient gum trees. Gloria sat alone trying not to cry while pretending to study her little tub of sliced melon and strawberries.

She noticed a black beetle crawling drunkenly over the grass, its movements slow and clumsy as though it were out of place in the vast sea of green. She watched its progression through blurry eyes, blinking furiously to stop the tears from falling. She missed her old school in Melbourne, and her friends Emily and Reena. She knew that time was different in Perth and her friends were probably in music class now, thinking about home-time.

The beetle rolled onto its back, its tiny legs cycling in the air. She considered turning it over, but the thought of touching it made her skin feel weird. A shadow fell across the grass, sending the beetle into darkness. Gloria frowned and looked up, expecting to see clouds gathering in the crystal blue sky, instead there stood Rhetty.

Momentarily blinded by the sun, all Gloria could see was her outline: short, slightly plump, and swathed in a navy-blue tunic. Gloria squared her shoulders and lifted her chin. If the girl standing over her said or did something mean, Gloria wanted to be ready with what she hoped would be an equally mean come back.

"Hi, I'm Harriet. Harriet Breckley."

Gloria raised a hand to shield her eyes from the glare. With the sun partially blocked, the shape coalesced, revealing a smiling girl with blonde pigtails. She crossed her sandaled feet at the ankles and dropped into a sitting position.

"You're pretty," Harriet said. Then, leaning closer, "I've got a chocolate brownie, do you want some?"

Gloria hesitated, wondering if it was some sort of trick. Would the girl wait for her to reach for the brownie then snatch it away and laugh? Before she could answer, the girl broke the brownie in two and handed her a chunk.

"Go ahead. It's really yummy. My mum made it," she said, waving the chunk of brownie in front of Gloria's eyes.

"Thanks." She took a bite and smiled. It *was* yummy; gooey on the inside and crunchy on the outside.

"I'm Gloria," she managed to say through a mouthful of chocolate.

"I know. Mrs. Trisk introduced you to the class, remember?" Harriet smiled again, and shoved her half of the brownie into her mouth. "When we go back to class, I'll ask her if you can sit with me, if you like."

Gloria felt an overwhelming wave of gratitude. She wanted to laugh, but for some strange reason tears popped into her eyes. She didn't want Harriet to see her upset or she might think Gloria a cry baby and not want to keep talking to her. She looked down at her fruit and blinked as fast as her eyes would move. When she felt sure the tears were gone she looked up to find Harriet studying her. There were tears in the other girl's eyes.

"It's okay," she whispered, putting her hand on Gloria's arm. "Now that we're friends, you don't have to be upset."

For a moment they said nothing, and then Harriet broke the spell. "Ooh, is that melon? Can I have some?"

* * *

"Will you help me?"

33

The words brought Gloria back from her reverie. She looked around the bar and saw jagged streaks of sunlight struggling to penetrate the blacked-out windows. She looked across at Rhetty and realised her friend's pain. The burden of what they'd done had begun to destroy her.

"Of course I'll help you," Gloria said and reached across the scarred table.

Rhetty clutched her hand as though she were grabbing a lifeline, but her fingers were light, as if lacking strength.

"I know things haven't been the same since … Well, since that night, but I'm still here for you. You're the only family I have." As her words tumbled out, Gloria realised she meant it.

"Thank you." Rhetty gave Gloria's hand a squeeze before releasing it. She grabbed her bag and slid from the booth.

"What now?" Gloria asked.

Rhetty stopped and gave her an incredulous look. "We go back to Herron," she said as though it were the most obvious thing in the world.

Chapter Six

Gloria sat on the icy tiles, her knees drawn up in an attempt to shield herself. She pressed her fist to her chest and realised her top was still hiked up around her neck. She pulled it down and wrapped both arms around her knees. Her body shook; it started somewhere deep in her stomach and spread up her back and down her legs until her entire body spasmed.

Blasts of music hit her as the bathroom door opened and closed. She heard voices, footsteps, and laughter as people moved around her. Her teeth were chattering, the sound hollow and jarring. She felt so cold her feet were numb.

Closing her eyes, she put her head on her knees, making herself as small as possible, crouched underneath the farthest wall-mounted sink opposite the toilet stalls. If she could make herself into a tiny ball, maybe no one would see her. She needed sleep – wanted to find the soft blackness and crawl into it, but something kept pulling her back.

A hand squeezed her shoulder. Gloria's eyes flew open. She tried to scream, but her mouth only opened and closed. She pulled away, darting to the left on bruised knees.

Not again.

Her left hand smacked against the tiles and her knees slid back and forth trying to find purchase on the slippery floor.

"Gloria! Gloria, please. Gloria it's me, Rhetty. Gloria, look at me."

She stopped struggling and turned towards the voice. Unsure if it was real, but desperately hoping it was.

"Rhetty?" The word was an effort; it came out on a laboured breath.

Gloria looked up at Rhetty surrounded by a halo of the overhead light. She reached out and grabbed her friend's arm.

Rhetty knelt and Gloria felt herself encircled by her friend's embrace. The heat of Rhetty's body wrapped around her like a soft blanket as the clean smell of apples filled her nose. Gloria leaned her head onto Rhetty's shoulder and closed her eyes.

A burst of music and a blast of hot air filled the room. Rhetty pulled away and jumped to her feet. Gloria watched as her friend slammed the bathroom door and dragged the metal rubbish bin in front. Someone pounded on the door. Gloria whimpered, drawing her knees back up to her chest.

"Hey. I need to use the toilet. Let me in!" A woman's voice from the other side of the door sounded slurred and angry.

"My friend's just vomited everywhere. Give me a few minutes to clean up the worst of it."

No response. Rhetty moved back to Gloria.

"We need to get you out of here." Rhetty slid her arms under Gloria's.

Gloria managed to stand. Her legs shook, but the violent spasms seemed to have stopped.

"Let's go." Rhetty pulled her towards the door.

Gloria resisted.

Rhetty turned back with a questioning look. Gloria raised her right hand, still balled into a fist. She turned it palm up and opened it.

"Oh, Gloria," she whispered, and her shoulders slumped. She took the pair of black lace underwear and stooped down. "Here, lean on me and I'll help you put them on."

Gloria placed her hands on her friend's shoulders. She stepped awkwardly into the underwear, much as a young child would. Without a word, Rhetty pulled up the pants and then took off her jacket. She held it up and Gloria gratefully slipped into it.

Gloria looked down into Rhetty's face. The lighting in the bathroom glowed harsh and unfiltered, but there was no mistaking the sadness there. Just for an instant, before her friend turned away, Gloria thought she saw something else, maybe disgust flicked across Rhetty's gaze.

"Come on. I'm taking you to Herron. You'll feel better after a shower and a good night's sleep." Rhetty slid strands of hair back from Gloria's face. She touched the back of her head and Gloria winced. Rhetty pulled her hand away and they both stared at her fingers.

Blood, stark and red under the harsh lights.

"What happened to your head?" Rhetty asked, her voice beginning to rise.

"I ..." Gloria hesitated. Images of the sink and the memory of the stench flashed in her mind. "I don't know. I must have bumped it. Please, let's just get out of here."

Rhetty looked like she wanted to say something else, but changed her mind. She nodded and pushed the bin away. Then, slipping her arm through Gloria's, she used her other hand to pull the door open. Three girls waited to get into the bathroom. Gloria's eyes flickered across the group; she was sure she saw knowing smiles on their faces. She fixed her eyes on the carpet and allowed Rhetty to lead her through the crowd.

Rhetty shoved open the exit and they stumbled out into the parking lot. There were several groups of people standing around in clusters talking and smoking. Gloria sucked in the night air. She felt light-headed, as though standing on top of a mountain. Rhetty stopped and turned to her.

"Are you okay?"

Gloria let out a shuddering breath and nodded. "Yes. Much better now that I'm outside. I just needed some air." She hoped her voice sounded normal.

"What happened in there?"

"It doesn't matter." Gloria pulled her arm free and walked towards the passenger side of Rhetty's black Mazda. Her legs were still wobbly, but at least she didn't feel like she might fall at every step.

She wanted to get in the car and go as far away from the Easy Eight as possible. Waiting for Rhetty to unlock the doors lasted an eternity. Gloria couldn't help glancing over her shoulder every few seconds and scanning the parking lot. *He said his name was Smiley.* She looked around and towards the entrance to the bar. *Smiley.* Gloria felt the spasms build in her stomach again.

"I'll get in the back. I want to lie down." She climbed in and reached out to close the door when Rhetty stopped her.

"What did you take, Gloria?"

Gloria looked down into her lap and raked her fingers through her hair. She didn't want to tell Rhetty where she got the stuff, it would only lead to more questions and arguments. She wanted to lie down, close her eyes, and pretend that tonight never happened. Perhaps if she did that for long enough she'd be able to forget. Maybe when she opened her eyes, this night would be over and the nightmare would end.

"I don't know what I took." She watched Rhetty's mouth drop in disbelief. "I mean just a couple of pills ... Maybe ecstasy." She realised she wasn't making it any better.

Rhetty shook her head and slammed the door. Gloria watched her friend stomp around to the driver's side. After everything that had happened, Rhetty's disappointment hurt the most. If she found out what really happened in the ladies' room, her disappointment would turn to disgust; and right now, Gloria couldn't bare it.

Rhetty opened the door and sat behind the wheel. She hesitated before starting the car.

"I've got your clutch. I put it in my bag when you were dancing with that guy." She seemed to be waiting for a reply.

"Thanks."

"You of all people shouldn't be taking God knows what pills and drinking."

"I know," Gloria whispered.

Rhetty sighed and started the car. Gloria took one last look at the bar as they pulled away. The people who'd been standing outside the building had disappeared back inside. Suddenly the crowded, noisy bar seemed isolated and menacing. The light escaping around the windows and doors glowed an eerie blue, it seemed to reach out towards the car. For one crazy moment, Gloria thought it might curl around the back of the Mazda and suck them back again.

When they reached the exit and turned onto the road, Gloria let out a breath she hadn't realised she'd been holding. Lying her head down on the seat, she closed her eyes, content to let the night take her away.

Chapter Seven

March 4th 2015

Gloria flicked on the indicator and turned out of the Easy Eight parking lot, relieved to see the bar disappear in the rearview mirror. She glanced at the display, it was almost 4:00 pm. She and Rhetty had been in the bar for almost two hours. *Were we really talking for that long?* She tried to recount their conversation, but couldn't remember much of what had happened in the bar. *Maybe my brain doesn't want to remember anything that happened in the Easy Eight.*

"Do you think we should put this off for another day?" Gloria asked, glancing over at Rhetty. "It's getting late. We'll probably hit some peak-hour traffic on the way. Might not get there until nearly six."

"So?" Rhetty shrugged. "Do you have somewhere else to be?"

There was nothing to stop Gloria from driving to Herron. She had no plans and no one waiting for her. Sometimes she wondered what she did have, apart from money. When her parents died, she'd had Rhetty and for a while that had been enough. But four years ago their relationship changed, and since then Gloria had been alone. Sure, she'd been out on dates, but hadn't been able to let anyone get close to her, not since that night in the Easy Eight.

"No. I don't have anywhere to be."

They drove on in silence for a while. Gloria found herself thinking about the last time they drove to Herron together. It was the night Joanna died. *No, it was the night I killed her.*

Most of it remained a blur, but some parts burned her mind like an ugly scar. Those dark hulking memories she'd pushed to the back of her conscience and with them, all the details of that night. But since entering the Easy Eight things started flittering in and out of focus. She remembered Rhetty finding her in the bathroom, the flood of relief and gratitude, but something didn't sit right. Something she couldn't put her finger on.

"You said you saw Joanna," she said, breaking the silence.

"What?"

Gloria glanced over at Rhetty whose gaze remained fixed on the road ahead.

"You said Joanna was back. You saw her walking along the road," Gloria waited for a response.

"Yes. I saw her."

"Well? What happened?"

It took Rhetty a minute or so to answer. Gloria kept stealing glances at her while trying to focus on the road. Something about the way Rhetty kept staring straight ahead, and her hesitation, made Gloria wonder if she was being completely honest. When Rhetty began talking about Joanna being back, Gloria didn't believe it, but she could tell Rhetty believed what she was saying. Now, she wasn't so sure.

"I saw her in the road, just like I said. *Say My Name* was playing on the radio and … and I pulled over and got out of my car. I tried to run after her, but a car came towards me and the lights blinded me." She turned her head towards the passenger window so Gloria could no longer even see her profile. "When I could see again, she was gone. The road, empty as if she'd never been there."

"But you're sure it was her?"

"It was her." Rhetty turned and faced Gloria. "I know what I saw, Gloria." She turned back to the window.

"Why do we need to go to Herron? What do you expect to find there?" Gloria gripped the wheel hard enough to turn her knuckles white.

"It's where this started. I think it's where she wants to finish it," she said softly, almost to herself.

Finish it?

Gloria didn't know what that meant, but she didn't like the sound of it. Meeting Rhetty today, drinking at the Easy Eight, and now *this*. A thought played on the edges of her mind like a half-remembered song, but before she could grasp it, the memory vanished leaving a hazy trail of confusion. The building dread in Gloria's chest swelled. Her mind kept coming back to the night all this started. Years of suppressed memories bubbled to the surface.

"Why didn't you take me to the hospital?" It was a question that nagged Gloria since they'd left the bar. Until today it had never occurred to her that when Rhetty found her in the ladies' room, the most logical thing to do would've been exactly that. So why hadn't she?

"What?"

"That night, when you found me in the ladies' room, why didn't you take me to the hospital?"

The silence stretched out between them until it seemed Rhetty wasn't going to answer.

"I thought about it, but you were *so* wasted. I knew there'd be questions you wouldn't want to answer."

"I had a head injury. It could've been serious. With my history… Anything could have happened."

"Every day of my life I think about that night and I wish I'd done things differently," Rhetty said, turning to face her. "If I'd taken you to the hospital or if we'd gone home instead of driving to Herron, things would be different. My life wouldn't be… Joanna would still be alive." She shook her head. "Don't you think I know that?"

"Okay. Sorry. I don't know why I brought it up." Gloria managed a weak smile, reached over and patted her friend's arm. Her skin was cold.

They were on the freeway heading towards Mandurah. It would be at least another hour until they reached Herron. Gloria had visited her holiday house regularly over the last four years. Far from making her hate the place, what happened there that night seemed to glue her to it. She often spent days there sleeping, reading, or just sitting staring at the water. But the thought of returning with Rhetty set her nerves on edge. She couldn't shake the execrable feeling of dread.

Chapter Eight

March 5th 2011

Gloria woke to the slamming of the car door. She inhaled a sharp breath; her heart thudded an uneven beat. For a moment, she was back in the ladies' room with the smell of metal and soap filling her nose and mouth. Then her thoughts cleared. *I'm in Rhetty's car. They're gone and I'm in the car.*

She sat up and a wave of dizziness hit. Her stomach roiled, bile rose up in her throat. She scrambled for the door, managed to open it and fall out of the car in time to vomit a stream of acrid bile. She used the car door as leverage and pulled herself up. Once on her feet, her ankles felt loose, almost numb. She stumbled forward and stepped in the foul-smelling liquid. It splashed her right shoe and ankle, the sight and feel of it brought on another fit of vomiting.

When her stomach finally stopped cramping, Gloria dragged the back of her hand across her mouth and looked around. The street sat shrouded in darkness but for the light spilling from the shopfront across the road. The sign over the shop read Bottle O' Rum. Gloria recognised the liquor shop from previous years when she and Rhetty had stopped off for last minute supplies.

Gloria stood wringing her hands. *Why was Rhetty taking so long?* Outside of the arc of light from the open car door, the blackness was broken only by the faint yellow glow from the liquor shop window. *I could go and wait in the shop, just stand inside the door near the counter until Rhetty's finished.* But inside, the shop was brightly lit. The clerk would see her and he'd know what had happened to her. *He'd see it on my face, smell it on me.* She struggled to breathe past another wave of nausea. Glancing up and down the empty street, she wondered if someone was crouching in the shadows; maybe watching her right now. The men from the bar could've followed them, waiting for her to be alone.

Headlights flooded the street and a car drove towards her.

She realised that with the door open, she stood in a pool of light. The car drew closer and seemed to slow. Gloria slid back into the vehicle and slammed the door. She crouched down below the window and waited.

Lights filled the car.

Her heart hammered her chest; thwunck, thwunck, thwunck. She heard a woman's voice and bit down on her fist to keep from screaming. Laughter. She held her breath, waiting.

The car lights moved away and slowly disappeared. Gloria let out a long shaky sigh. She started to raise her head to risk a look out the window when the driver's door flung open and light flooded the car. Gloria let out an agonised cry and dove for the door nearest her. She managed to get her hand on the release lever when someone grabbed her shoulder.

"Gloria! Gloria, stop it!"

She let go of the lever and turned around. Rhetty rested on her knees, leaning around the driver's seat. Her face looked yellow and shadowed under the car's interior light.

"Gloria, what's the matter with you? You're acting crazy."

She tried to answer but relief and exhaustion turned her response into a series of hiccupping sobs.

"It's okay," Rhetty's tone softened. "Everything's okay. I just went in the liquor shop to grab some supplies."

"Sorry," Gloria managed to stutter out. "I – I just woke-up and got a bit disorientated. That's all."

Rhetty stared at her for a moment. "Put my jacket back on, you're shivering." She turned away and sat behind the wheel.

* * *

They drove in silence, Gloria watching the back of Rhetty's head, like that of a dummy in a shop window, stiff and frozen. *Was she angry? Disapproving? Disgusted?* Rhetty turned on the radio and noise spilled from the speakers cancelling the silence. Gloria pulled Rhetty's jacket around her shoulders and leaned her head back, listening to the soft music as it filled the car.

She didn't really want to go to Herron. Not tonight. But if she asked Rhetty to take her home, her friend would be disappointed, and Gloria would have to spend the night alone. She decided to go along with the trip and then tell

Rhetty she felt sick. She'd take a long, hot shower and then crawl into bed.

"I love this song," Rhetty said over her shoulder and turned up the volume.

Gloria smiled to herself and listened to Rhetty sing *Say My Name*, repeating the three words over and over. Gloria looked out the window and up at the black expanse. There was something otherworldly about the way the stars sparkled in the West Australian sky.

She remembered her father had once said Perth was the most isolated city in the world and that everything here seemed bigger and more real. He'd said that when he looked at the night sky, it was easy to believe the rest of the world had vanished.

What would he think of me now? For the first time in her life, Gloria felt glad he'd died and couldn't see what a mess she'd become.

"There's someone walking in the road." Rhetty's voice cut through the mist of Gloria's memories.

"Probably a drunk." Gloria leaned forward to get a better look.

Thirty metres ahead, just off the curb, the headlights illuminated a figure. As they drew nearer, Rhetty slowed the car.

"What are you doing? You're not going to stop, are you?"

"I think it's … it's Joanna." Rhetty pulled the car over to the curb.

For a moment both women watched the figure. A car passed, going in the opposite direction, its lights joining Rhetty's and flooding the street. The figure became clearer, a woman's shape came into view, but Gloria couldn't be sure who it was. Rhetty beeped the horn and the woman turned. She held her hand up to her face to block the glare. Gloria could make out the woman's silhouette and dark spiky hair. She walked towards the car, bathed in the beam of yellow light.

Gloria's stomach dropped. Joanna stood in front of the car, one hand on her hip, head cocked to the side.

"You said she was only having drinks with us," Gloria hissed at Rhetty from the back seat.

"I don't know what she's doing here, but I'm going to find out."

Before Gloria could protest, Rhetty jumped out of the car. *Say my name, say my name. You actin' kind of shady.* Gloria lowered her window and leaned her head out so she could hear what the two women were saying. The smell of burnt petrol filled her nose as she watched them embrace. From what she could hear, Joanna had planned to meet someone who never showed up.

The conversation sounded forced. Gloria had no doubt that they'd staged it for her benefit. Did Rhetty really want Joanna with them so badly that she would go these lengths? *Or, maybe she just doesn't want to be stuck with me for the night.*

Gloria put the window up and leaned back. She couldn't really blame Rhetty, Joanna was manipulative and Gloria had played right into her hands getting *so* wasted. As much as she hated the thought of having Joanna in her house, maybe it would work out for the best. At least when Gloria said she didn't feel well and went to bed, Rhetty wouldn't be left alone.

"Fancy meeting you here," Joanna said climbing into the front passenger seat.

"Funny how things turn out," Gloria snapped.

Joanna gave a forced laugh and turned away.

Rhetty got back in and leaned around the driver's seat. She put her hand on Gloria's leg. "Joanna's friend stood her up so she was walking home. I asked her to come with us and spend the night in Herron. I said you wouldn't mind." She glanced at Joanna.

Gloria wanted to tell Rhetty that she *did* mind. That the last thing she wanted after what she'd been through, was to spend the night with Joanna. She wanted to insist that Rhetty chose between her and Joanna, but a scared little voice inside her head warned that, if she forced the issue, maybe she wouldn't like Rhetty's choice.

"Yes. That's fine," she said, and gave Rhetty a weak smile.

"Thanks, Gloria." Rhetty gave Gloria's knee a quick squeeze and turned back to the road. She put the car in drive and pulled out.

Gloria leaned back and closed her eyes. *Will this night ever end?*

Chapter Nine

March 4ᵗʰ 2015

With Mandurah behind them, Gloria crossed the Dawesville Cut Bridge and turned onto Old Coast Road. As always, the beauty of the place struck her. She glanced over at Rhetty, rather than warming her features, the afternoon sun made her look almost colourless, like a faded image in an old photograph. Gloria frowned and quickly turned her attention back to the view.

The Dawesville Channel lay on her left. It was also known as the Cut, a man-made channel that connects the Peel-Harvey Estuary and the Indian Ocean; clear blue water and narrow white sandy beaches on one side, spacious homes with rolling lawns on the other. This was 'Old Dawesville' where people came to retire or holiday. A place of tranquillity that Gloria hadn't found elsewhere.

"I never get tired of this place," she said, more to herself than Rhetty.

"I know," Rhetty answered still looking out the passenger window. Gloria couldn't blame her for being taken with the view. The Cut was breathtaking, particularly as evening approached and the trees cast their long shadows across the water.

Gloria checked the time – 5:50 pm. They should reach the house in less than fifteen minutes. *What then?* Did Rhetty really think Joanna's ghost would be waiting for them? Gloria didn't believe in ghosts, but if she did, she guessed Joanna's would be pissed. She looked down and released her white-knuckled grip on the wheel.

She turned and looked at the water instead. A group of people waded through the shallows, a large black dog paddling behind them. Their bodies cast rippling shadows across the water. They carried long-handled scoop nets. The image reminded her of childhood: walking through the water with her dad while her mother watched from the shore. Her mother's occasional warning, "Watch your step, Gloria." Every step became an adventure because at any moment a crab might nip your toe. Even with running shoes, the large blue manna crabs could reach up and pinch your ankle.

Gloria wished she could stop the car and watch the group hunt for crabs. She considered suggesting the idea to Rhetty, but dismissed it just as fast. They weren't here to while away the hours in the setting sun.

"The phone you showed me, you said you found it in your garden?" Gloria paused and waited for Rhetty to comment. When she didn't respond, Gloria continued. "How did it get there?"

"I told you. Joanna."

"That doesn't explain it. Or are you saying you think Joanna's ghost buried her phone in your back yard?"

"We're nearly there," Rhetty said with a forced brightness.

For almost the entire journey, Rhetty had been like a ghost herself, but now she came alive – as if the close proximity to the house gave her energy.

It made Gloria uneasy. The whole idea of being in Herron with Rhetty made her uneasy. *Of course it does, the last time I was here with her turned into a nightmare. It's natural that being back in the house together is a little freaky.*

She turned her attention back to the road. The houses dropped away, replaced by bush on both sides. They entered a tunnel of tall gum trees and an understorey dense with small trees, shrubs, and grasses. On the left Gloria caught the occasional glimpse of the estuary between massive swaths of bush which encroached onto both sides of the road; the sun that struggled through the trees here was drenched in sinopia shadows, allowing only the darkest light to filter through.

"That night," Gloria said suddenly. "You and Joanna planned it didn't you?" Looking over at Rhetty, she could see she had her full attention now.

"Planned what?"

"For Joanna to be on the road when we passed. For us to stop and pick her up. I heard you talking to someone when I woke-up in the car. It was her. You were on the phone with *her*, weren't you?"

"You're paranoid. You were then, and you are now," Rhetty snapped.

In all the years she'd known her, Rhetty had been the level-headed voice of reason: kind, bubbly, gentle. Now, the cruel edge in her tone made Gloria's insides shrivel. And then, as if Rhetty sensed her thoughts, she softened.

"I worry about you sometimes, are you taking your medication?"

"I … I. No. I don't need it any more, I'm fine." Gloria tried not to sound as hurt as she felt. She was doing this for Rhetty. Because Rhetty had said *she* needed help. Now she'd turned it around making Gloria feel like the fragile one again. She wondered what her life would be like if, when Rhetty's shadow fell on her all those years ago at school, she'd refused her offer of friendship. Gloria almost certainly would never have met Joanna.

She immediately felt guilty for thinking such a thing. Rhetty had always been her closest and dearest friend. Whatever path their lives had taken couldn't be blamed on Rhetty just because she'd befriended Gloria when they were kids.

"Look, Rhetty, I'm sorry I keep asking questions." She paused, searching for the right words. "It's just that, you know, sometimes my memory gets a bit foggy and … well, being back here with you is stirring everything up. I'm just trying to make sense of what we're doing here."

"It's okay, really, and I'm sorry I snapped at you. I guess we're here to try and figure out what Joanna wants, and how we can put things right." Rhetty shook her head. "It doesn't make much sense, I know, but I need you to trust me."

Gloria smiled and let go of the wheel just long enough to give Rhetty's small hand a gentle pat. The strange moment had passed, but try as she might, she couldn't shake the feeling that her time with Rhetty was coming to an end.

Chapter Ten

March 5th 2011

Street lights this far out of the city were non-existent. The only light came from the twin orbs of the headlamps and the silvery moonlight that clawed its way through the dense crop of trees and bush. Occasionally they passed a house, always on the left facing the water. They were on Southern Estuary Road where houses rose on huge blocks carved out of the bush and abutted the water. In contrast to the wild, untamed vegetation around them, the homes sat on rolling lawns, often with tennis courts or sprawling gardens.

"Jesus. I had no idea this place even existed," Joanna said as they passed an imposing stone-and-steel home set back from the road by a curving, crushed-brick driveway.

Rhetty laughed. A soft chuckle that Gloria had come to recognise over the years as her you-ain't-seen-nothing-yet laugh. Gloria usually liked the laugh; it meant that

Rhetty was about to tell a really funny story or juicy piece of gossip, but tonight it seemed ominous.

"What about the neighbours?" Joanna asked.

"Gloria's house sits on a five-acre block," Rhetty said with another little chuckle. "We are guaranteed absolute privacy."

Gloria frowned and winced as the cut on her head moved a fraction. She wondered why Joanna cared about the neighbours. Then her heart beat faster. *What if Joanna had invited someone else along? The men from the bar? 'Call me Smiley.'*

"Why are you asking about the neighbours? Have you told someone to meet you here?" The question came out as a panicked croak.

"Relax," Joanna said turning. "I just meant that if we have a few drinks and go for a swim, we might get loud. We don't want anyone getting the wrong idea and calling the cops, do we?"

Gloria took a few deep breaths and forced herself to calm down. They were in Herron. Her safe place. Nothing bad could happen here.

"How's your head?" Rhetty asked and locked eyes with her in the rear vision mirror.

"It's been worse," Gloria said, and they both laughed.

Suddenly Gloria felt better. Rhetty hadn't changed: she was still the only person who really knew her. They'd been through so much together, how could she have thought Rhetty's friendship with Joanna would change that closeness?

"What's so funny?" Joanna asked.

Gloria smiled to herself, pleased that she and Rhetty still had 'in' jokes that Joanna could never really get. She was about to tell Joanna it was nothing when, to her horror, Rhetty explained.

"When Gloria was seventeen, she had a major car accident. She had some really bad head injuries that left her in a coma for six days." Rhetty paused and looked over her shoulder at Gloria. "We were lucky she survived."

Gloria felt the heat creep up her neck and a small finger of anger uncurl inside her stomach. They discussed her life so freely. *Her* tragedy. *Her* sorrow.

"God, Gloria. That's heavy," Joanna said turning to look at her.

Gloria clenched her jaw and looked down at her hands; they were balled into fists.

"Was anyone else hurt?" Joanna persisted.

Gloria didn't answer. She closed her eyes and prayed Rhetty wouldn't either.

"Gloria's father. He died in the crash."

"Oh … I'm sorry, Gloria. That must have been tough." Joanna's voice trailed off and she fell silent.

The air felt thick, suffocating. The weight of it pinned her in the back seat under Joanna's scrutiny. The pity and judgement in the woman's voice made her feel sick. After everything that had happened tonight, the torture kept on coming.

She wanted to scream. Scream at Joanna, but more than that she wanted to scream at Rhetty. How could she reveal the most painful moments of Gloria's life to this stranger? Instead of screaming, she said nothing and let the anger build.

"Here it is!" Rhetty sang triumphantly.

The headlights swept a tunnel of yellow along the crushed red-brick driveway. The car's bonnet rocked up slightly and then dipped as the house came into view.

A single storey stone–and-timber structure rose out of the blackness like a tombstone. Rhetty edged the car closer to the house, activating the sensor lights. The glow pooled in three wide arcs, bringing the façade into focus. Six large windows gleamed obsidian in the moonlight. Large, double doors of dark wood cut the house down the middle.

Gloria let out a sigh of relief and climbed out of the car. She stood, wobbled to the left and grabbed the door for support. In spite of the house's imposing gothic look, it was the closest thing to home she had left. When they first moved to Perth, her father had the house built on her mother's family land. Her parents worked with the architect to create a house that was spacious, comfortable and unique to the area.

She'd spent many happy and bittersweet times here. Long summer days crabbing, swimming, or jetting around in the boat with her parents; her father always gentle and funny, and her mother confident and smiling.

Then there were the months leading up to her mother's death. Her father decided it would be better for her mum's health if they left the city for a while and stayed at the Herron house. *The Herron house*, that's what he'd always called it. Being here usually made her feel close to her parents, but tonight she felt small and alone.

"Well? Are we going in?" Joanna asked, slamming the car door. She stood with her hands on her hips and surveyed the house. "Creepy but cool." She threw Gloria a wink.

Gloria ignored her and turned to Rhetty, who unloaded a cardboard box out of the boot. "You said you had my bag?"

Rhetty nodded towards the car, "It's in the front on the floor."

Gloria turned to retrieve the bag when Rhetty stopped her. "Wait, Gloria. How's your head? Are you feeling any better?"

"Do you care?" Gloria snapped. The anger bubbling away inside her while Rhetty flippantly discussed her accident with Joanna, now boiled to the surface. "How could you tell her?"

"Gloria, I —"

Gloria held up her hand. "No! You know how I feel about the accident. You know I never talk about it, and yet you told *her*."

Rhetty dumped the box back in the boot and grabbed Gloria's arm. "Please, Gloria. I'm sorry. I didn't mean anything. I just ... well I guess I'm just grateful that I still have you and we're all here together. I got a bit excited." Rhetty's chin trembled and tears welled on her lower lids. "Please, say you'll forgive me?"

Gloria knew she should feel guilty for turning on Rhetty, but all she wanted was to get away from her. The thought surprised her. Then another quickly followed. *Maybe our friendship has run its course?*

"Yes, of course," Gloria said trying to sound convincing. And then added, "I'm just exhausted."

"Not too exhausted to have one drink with us, I hope?" Joanna asked from behind her.

"Okay. One drink," Gloria said with a stiff smile. *But in the morning I want you both out of my life.*

Chapter Eleven

Gloria turned the key and pushed the double doors open. She tossed the fob and bag on the hall table and headed towards the sitting room. The house was a network of shadows. At almost 6:00 pm all that remained of the sun was diminishing streaks across the stone floor. Gloria moved through the house opening blinds and turning on lamps, her heels making a click-clack sound on the floor. She felt Rhetty's presence behind her.

When Gloria reached the French doors that led to the back deck, she drew the curtains.

"Look at that, Rhetty. I love the way the sky turns two kinds of orange before the sun sets."

The view from the main room was breathtaking: in front of them sat a large expanse of deck; wide stone stairs cut a line down the centre of the area and led to the pool; in front of the pool, lush green lawn eventually became a narrow stretch of white sand that met the water's edge; on either side of the expanse, natural bush circled them.

For a few moments, they stood shoulder to shoulder watching the vermilion sky. Gloria found her gaze drawn to the pool. She quickly turned away.

"I'll make us some coffee," she said, and headed for the kitchen.

In the centre of the kitchen sat a large island. Gloria bent and grabbed the coffee cups from under the grey and black marble top and set them on the counter. Turning, she took the kettle from the bench that formed a semi-circle around the room. She filled it using the tap in the double sink, set it back in its original spot, and turned it on.

The mundane task of making coffee felt comfortable and, for the first time since this strange day began, her nerves settled. Her stomach growled and she realised all she'd eaten that day was a slice of brown toast at breakfast. *Is there any food in the house?* The last time she was here was … *when?*

She rubbed the heels of her hands against her temples, a little habit she'd developed after the car accident. It helped her focus, grab onto memories when they tried to scurry away. After the accident, the doctor had told her that the memories were all there, she just had to use a different path to find them.

Last Wednesday, she thought triumphantly. She'd come to meet Ron. Ronald Brackett and his wife Linda were caretakers of sorts. They lived locally and managed a number of holiday houses in Herron and Dawesville. Ron looked after the garden and minor maintenance while Linda cleaned the house once a fortnight. Ron had called her about the pool pump. She smiled to herself as the memory returned.

Gloria spooned instant coffee into the cups. Last time she visited Herron, she put a bag of green apples in the fridge and a box of chocolate chip cookies in the pantry. For a second she considered the two. After a brief hesitation, she decided to grab both. She opened the pantry, pleased to see her memory hadn't let her down. The box of cookies sat on the shelf where she'd left them.

With the coffee made, Gloria reached under the bench and took out a small blue plate. She opened the box, placed three cookies on the dish and one in her mouth. She ate it in two bites then turned to retrieve an apple and stopped. A message caught her eye, scrawled on the whiteboard she kept on the fridge.

She frowned and stared at the words. It was her handwriting, but she had no memory of writing it. *Your memory is getting worse,* a voice in her head whispered and a shiver crawled its way up her spine. It wasn't the usual appointment reminder or shopping list. Just three words: *Check your journal.*

"Do you need any help?"

Gloria spun around surprised. "I didn't hear you come in."

Rhetty smiled and motioned towards the fridge. "I didn't know you still kept a journal."

"I don't." Gloria didn't know why she was lying. "Not a proper one anyway. More of an appointment book with reminders. You know, to help with my memory." She turned away from the fridge. Suddenly she wasn't hungry and the headache that started when she arrived at the Easy Eight, ramped up into a sullen throb.

"I thought you said you stopped taking your medication because you didn't need it anymore," Rhetty said, still staring at the message on the fridge.

Gloria picked up the coffees, ignoring the question. "Shall we have these on the deck?"

* * *

Gloria leaned back and took a sip of coffee; it was hot and bitter. The air, redolent with the smell of salt water and damp wood complimented the sky which turned from burnt orange to purple. It reminded Gloria of a line in a poem, *rage against the dying of the light*. She couldn't remember the poet's name, but that line resonated with her. Maybe because she'd lost the two people closest to her, or maybe because she'd seen the dying of the light – in Joanna's eyes.

She turned to look at Rhetty who sat staring down at the pool, her coffee cup untouched on the table between them. The change in her friend unsettled her. She seemed shrunken, aged.

"We need to end this," Rhetty said tiredly.

Gloria set her cup down next to Rhetty's. "You said you saw Joanna. You said you talked to her, was any of that true?"

"You think I made it up? Why would I do that?"

"I don't know, Rhetty. I don't know why you wanted to come here. To raise the dead? Is that why?" Her voice started to rise. "Because I don't believe in ghosts."

"We came here to make you *understand*."

"Understand what?" Gloria didn't want to go down this path. If Rhetty insisted on going to the police, she didn't know what she'd do. She'd go to prison, that much she *was* sure of. It wouldn't matter what her reasons were, she had killed someone. Worse than that, she'd covered up her crime for the past four years. She rubbed her damp palms on the front of her dress.

"You can't go on like this, Gloria. You can't keep coming here pretending nothing happened."

Pretending, why did that word make her dizzy? "Why? After all this time, why can't you just let it rest?"

"Because," Rhetty motioned to the pool. "Joanna can't rest until you face up to what you've done. None of us can."

Gloria looked down at the pool. Night drew in, shrouding it in shadows. The water looked dark as ink. She could see something on its surface near the deep end. She sat forward in her seat, frowning, trying to make sense of what she saw.

"Oh my God," Gloria screamed and jumped to her feet. Her thigh collided with the corner of the table. A searing pain shot up her leg. The coffee cups clattered and rolled to their sides.

A body floated in the pool. Arms and legs spread wide, spiky hair floated around the head like a thorny halo. Terror billowed in Gloria's mind.

"It can't be."

Rhetty jumped to her feet next to Gloria. Gloria turned, her mouth open and eyes wide. Rhetty's face, unreadable in the dusk light stared back. Her fingers laced around Gloria's trembling arm and squeezed.

"Call the police."

Gloria shook head and snatched her arm away. "It can't be ... It must be someone else." Once the words were out, Gloria clung to them like a flickering glimmer of hope.

"Yes. It's someone else. They must have …" She looked around hoping to spot something. A towel, a pair of shoes. Anything that would indicate that the body in the pool wasn't Joanna's.

"We have to check." Gloria took a step towards the stairs.

"No." Rhetty grabbed her arm again. "Don't keep doing this."

Gloria didn't want to go down to the pool. She didn't want to see whoever floated in the water, but she had to be sure. It could be a stranger. *Not could be,* she corrected herself, *has to be.* It was the only explanation. *The dead don't come back,* she told herself. *What if they did? What if it is Joanna?*

The image of Joanna's dead milky eyes staring accusingly up at her from the water flashed in her mind.

"If you don't want to come with me, you can wait here." She pulled her arm away.

Gloria reached the stairs and started down. Her legs felt heavy as if she'd been sitting on them and they'd fallen asleep. She grabbed the railing to steady herself. Suddenly the warm evening air turned humid and breathing became difficult. She managed a deep gulp and swallowed. From this angle, she could see the shallow end of the pool, but not the body.

She took another step down and tried to crane her neck around to catch a glimpse of the dark thing in the water. A row of shaggy conifers on either side of the stairs made it impossible for her to see far enough. She hesitated, picturing Joanna's corpse standing on the other side of the bushes: yellow rotting flesh hanging from her outstretched arms, a knowing look in her eyes. Gloria grimaced and bit her lower lip hard enough to taste blood.

The light had nearly faded, throwing long shadows everywhere. Gloria cursed herself for not thinking to go inside and turn on the pool lights before coming down.

"Rhetty!" She winced at how loud her voice sounded in the empty garden. "Rhetty, turn on the pool lights."

Gloria waited. Nothing. Another thought occurred to her, one almost as frightening as facing the thing in the pool. *What if she's calling the police?*

It was enough to get her moving. Gloria let go of the railing and hurried down the last two steps. When her right foot touched the bottom, the left one caught on something. She sprawled forward and landed hard on her hands and knees.

"Fuck!"

Gloria struggled to her feet. Her palms and right knee burned. With Rhetty inside, maybe calling the police, she couldn't waste time examining her injuries. She had to pull the body out of the pool. *What if it's Joanna,* a voice inside whispered.

"It's not." *There has to be another explanation.* But whoever it was, she couldn't let the police find them in the pool.

She rounded the conifers. The smell of chlorine filled her nose. Without the pool lights, the near dark made it difficult to see. She looked up and back towards the house where warm yellow light filtered over the deck, but didn't quite reach the pool level. She considered going back and turning on the lights. *If I go back now, I won't have the courage to return.*

Gloria forced herself to walk forward. In the stillness, frogs croaked and crickets chirped – sounds of the fading summer. Underlying those familiar sounds came something else. She strained to hear, then recognising it, she took a step back and stopped. It was a wet sound. Water smacking against something. Her heart thundered in her throat and her breath came in sharp bursts.

Something floated in the pool. Something large and dark. She could see its form moving on the water. She took another step closer. Only a few metres away now, she could make out the details. The shape seemed inhuman, stiff. There was something odd about the way it moved in the water. Gloria clenched her fist around the neckline of her dress. She took a tentative step closer. Bending her knees, she leaned over the edge.

For a moment, she thought the fading light and her mounting fear played tricks on her. Then her mind caught up with reality and she realised what she was seeing: a fallen branch caught in the filter.

The strength drained from her body. Surrendering to the feeling, she sank to her knees and plunged her hands into her hair. *Is this what it feels like to go insane?* Maybe, because suddenly the situation struck her as comical and she laughed out loud.

* * *

By the time Gloria climbed back up to the deck, full darkness had fallen. The coffee cups lolled on their sides, their contents forming a brown pool that spread across the table and leaked over the side, staining the wood of the deck. She stopped and, without thinking, set the cups back in an upright position. The French doors stood open.

"Rhetty?" Gloria called and waited. When no answer came, she stepped through.

The house remained still, save the sounds of insects and night creatures echoing in from the bush. *Did Rhetty call the police?* If so, how much had she told them? The terror that had seized her going down to the pool dissipated, only to be replaced with a growing sense of panic.

She scanned the main room. Large, green, bespoke sofas formed an L-shape around a huge silk rug. At their meeting point sat a highly polished oak corner table. Gloria hesitated, her gaze drawn to the framed photograph on the table. Her own image smiled back at her.

She must have been about thirteen. Nestled between her parents, the three of them stood bathed in sunlight looking ridiculously happy. She remembered it as the last year she'd been truly happy.

Suddenly part of her wanted Rhetty to have called the police. *At least I'll have some peace. Some rest from the constant guilt and worry.*

Gloria sat down on the rug and stared at the photograph. She'd made so many mistakes. Done unforgivable things. Maybe it was time she was punished? Could that be what Rhetty wanted? To punish her? *We need to end this*, that's what Rhetty said. Gloria looked around the room and frowned. *What if Rhetty had meant something else when she said* end it*?*

Horrified, Gloria jumped to her feet. "Rhetty? Rhetty, where are you?" Her voice echoed in the empty house.

Heading for the front door she found it standing open and wondered if Rhetty had headed up to the road. It didn't make sense. She couldn't think of any reason for her to just walk away. The crescent moon offered little in the way of light.

Gloria stepped outside and the sensor lights came on. The car remained where she'd left it, so if Rhetty had gone, she was on foot. Sweat popped out on Gloria's neck and armpits. She jogged a few metres along the driveway before the combination of high heels and crushed gravel sent her into a skid. She stumbled, barely avoiding another fall.

The exit road was cloaked in darkness. Near the house, tall trees and thick scrub crowded the driveway. Gloria bit her lip, deepening the cut, and turned in a circle.

"Rhetty?" She called more out of desperation than any real hope of an answer.

Nothing.

She tasted blood in her mouth again. She spat onto the crushed brick and dragged the back of her hand across her mouth. It came away smeared with blood. Gloria looked around one last time. The bush was so dark and dense, it was easy to imagine something lurking behind it. Gloria turned and rushed back into the house.

Her handbag sat where she'd left it on the hall stand, *but where's Rhetty's bag?* She couldn't remember Rhetty putting it down. She shook her head and tried to picture what happened when they walked in. She felt sure Rhetty had trailed behind her, so for all Gloria knew she could've brought the bag with her to the main room.

Gloria trotted back to the main room and looked around.

Nothing.

She knew she was wasting time fixating on Rhetty's bag, when her friend might have done something desperate. *The bathroom!* She'd been so focused on Rhetty leaving the house, she hadn't considered the possibility she might be in one of the other rooms.

Rushing past the kitchen, she flicked on the hall lights. There were four bedrooms, two bathrooms, and a large laundry room in this part of the house. She cursed herself for being so slow. In the time it had taken her to go out front and stand there fretting, Rhetty could have hurt herself.

Gloria spent the next five minutes running from room to room, turning on lights and calling her friend's name. Finally, she came to the bathroom at the end of the hall. Next to the master bedroom, it was the larger of the two baths. Unlike the other rooms, the door was closed. Gloria couldn't see any light, but when she'd last seen Rhetty, the sun hadn't completely set. It was possible that Rhetty hadn't needed to turn on the lights to do whatever it was she planned on doing.

Gloria grabbed the handle. Her breath came in hard gasps. The grip felt slippery in her sweaty hand.

"Rhetty?"

She turned the knob.

Chapter Twelve

March 5th 2011

Gloria leaned across the driver's seat and let Rhetty's yellow blazer fall from around her shoulders. She could feel the heat thumping behind her eyes and recognised the beginnings of a migraine. The anger she'd felt when they arrived fizzled, leaving only weariness in its wake.

She scanned the floor on the passenger side and gave a sigh of relief when she spotted her clutch. The house keys were inside, and without them their only options were heading back to Perth or driving to Ron and Linda's house. Waking the elderly couple at midnight was the last thing she wanted to do, especially in her present state.

Backing out of the car, she noticed a phone in the console between the seats. Still crouched over, she picked it up. On the back of the case a cartoon face squinted with laughter. *Trust Joanna to think something this ugly could be cute.* The slit eyes and panting tongue looked ominous.

She lifted her head above the dashboard and took a quick glance around. Joanna and Rhetty waited near the front door. She turned the phone back over and looked at the screen. If it wasn't locked with a pass code, she could check the last call. If it was from Rhetty, it would prove they'd orchestrated this whole thing.

Another more frightening thought occurred to her. If she checked the messages, she might find proof that Joanna knew those men at the bar. *Then what?*

She couldn't waste time trying to come up with ideas, she had to get the phone inside and into her bedroom. She put her clutch on the driver's seat and flipped open the clasp.

"Oh, great. You found my phone." Joanna's voice made her jump.

Gloria backed out of the car and slapped the phone into the woman's outstretched hand. She watched as Joanna stuffed it into the front pocket of her pants. Joanna stood blocking Gloria's exit from the car. At 170 centimetres Gloria was far from short, but Joanna towered over her by a good ten centimetres.

Gloria thought of the way Joanna had grabbed her hand under the table at the Easy Eight. The woman's brown eyes had danced with pleasure at Gloria's pain. A similar predatory look lit them up now. Joanna wanted to hurt her again. Gloria didn't want to provoke the woman, but she refused to show any fear.

"Would you mind moving, I need to unlock the front door." Gloria hoped her tone carried a mixture of impatience and boredom.

Joanna smiled.

For a second it looked like she would stand her ground and refuse to let her pass. Gloria waited, holding eye contact with the woman. After what seemed like minutes, Joanna stepped aside and gestured for Gloria to pass. *I can't believe I'm about to let this woman into my house.*

* * *

Once inside, Gloria focused on turning on the lights. She walked through the main room and grabbed a dark-green throw from one of the sofas. She wrapped it around herself. The warm, comforting feel of soft cashmere only added to the feeling of weight on her skin. The weight of dirt and violation that made her want to scour her flesh until it was raw.

"Cold?" Rhetty asked, her face a mask of concern.

"A bit."

Gloria sat on the edge of the sofa.

Joanna walked around the room picking things up and examining them. She trailed her hand along the fitted bookshelves that lined the far-left wall. Then walked around the sofas and stood in front of the French doors.

"This place looks like something out of a magazine." She looked up at the high ceilings.

"I'm glad you approve," Gloria said sarcastically, and immediately regretted it.

She'd promised herself she wouldn't provoke the woman, but the thumping behind her eyes intensified, and something about the way Joanna stood – hands on hips, feet apart – inched its way under Gloria's skin. There was an air of ownership in the way she moved. She stopped and turned to look at Gloria. Her lips parted to say something, when Rhetty spoke first.

"I'll put this in the kitchen and make us some drinks." Rhetty nodded towards the box she held against her chest.

She seemed oblivious to the tension building between Gloria and Joanna. *Is she so naïve that she really believes I could ever be friends with Joanna? That or so spoilt she can't envision not getting her own way.* Gloria surprised herself by the bitterness she felt. Rhetty always got her own way; in fact, the end of summer celebrations had been Rhetty's idea. Gloria tried to remember how Rhetty had brought it up, but her mind clouded and the thudding ache slow-marched its way across her skull.

"Need help with the drinks?" Joanna asked, and followed Rhetty into the kitchen.

Gloria kicked off her heels – gold to match her top. She'd bought them a few days ago at a boutique in Mount Hawthorne. They were ridiculously expensive, but the sales woman had assured her that they made her legs look amazing. Now they were splattered with vomit. Just looking at them made her stomach lurch.

She picked up the shoes, taking care to only touch the heel straps. She could smell herself, a heavy mixture of sweat and sex. *Call me Smiley.* The words rang in her ears again. She needed a shower, to scrub herself until the smell and the memory washed away.

Gloria pulled the throw around her shoulders and padded down the hall, not bothering to turn on the lights. She slowed her footsteps and crossed to the far side as she passed the kitchen. Muffled voices and laughter filtered through, then the sound of the blender. Satisfied that they were preoccupied, she scurried towards the master bedroom.

"What are you doing?" Rhetty asked, her voice echoing down the hall.

Gloria stopped, frozen like an intruder in her own home. She'd hoped to grab her pyjamas and duck into the bathroom before Rhetty noticed she'd gone. Then, later when Rhetty and Joanna had had a few drinks, she'd say good night and this joyless party would be over.

"I thought you were going to have a drink with us?"

Gloria turned around, grateful for the lack of light. "Wow, Rhetty, will you stop acting like a mother hen? I'm just going to have a wash and put my pyjamas on. Is that alright?" Gloria tried to keep the tremor out of her voice.

"Yeah, Harriet, stop acting like a mother hen," Joanna called from the kitchen.

Rhetty didn't move, and for one horrifying second Gloria thought she was going to march down the hall and drag her into the kitchen. Then the moment evaporated and Rhetty laughed. She waved her hand.

"Sorry. I guess I am being a pain in the neck." She made a shooing gesture. "You go, I'll make you a cocktail and have it ready for when you come out."

Once in the bedroom, Gloria locked the door. She dropped her shoes on the floor and went to the double oak dresser that used to house her mother's clothes. She opened the second drawer, pulled out a pair of blue cotton pyjamas and tossed them on the bed. Over the last few years, she'd moved some of her things from the single bedroom she used as a child, into her parent's old room. It seemed strange at first, sleeping in their queen-sized bed, but at the same time comforting.

With Joanna just down the hall, the room seemed less soothing. Gloria threw the wrap on the bed and flopped down. She let her shoulders slump and put her head in her hands. The tears she'd been holding back flowed freely.

There was a time, not so long ago, when she would have turned to Rhetty. Told her what happened in the ladies' room, poured it all out. But things had changed. *Rhetty* had changed. *Or, maybe whatever pills Joanna sold me are making me crazy?*

She blew out a long shuddering breath and dragged the back of her hand across her wet skin. A mixture of warm tears and snot smeared her forearm. She closed her eyes and forced herself to breathe in and out slowly. After three breaths, the tears stopped. Gloria lifted the bottom of her silky gold top and wiped her eyes then let it drop back against her skin. With a Herculean effort, she stood and unlocked the door.

In her eagerness to get into the bathroom, she didn't notice the light under the door. Gloria slid her pyjamas under her arm and turned the knob. Holding the door ajar, she glanced back down the hall. She could hear cupboards being opened and glasses clinking. Joanna and Rhetty were starting the party without her.

Good. She hoped they'd get drunk and forget about her.

Still looking over her shoulder, Gloria stepped into the bathroom. She closed the door. It took a fraction of a second to grasp that the light was on and the bathroom occupied.

"What are you doing here?"

Joanna crouched in front of the double sinks going through the cupboards underneath. She ignored Gloria's question and continued her search. Gloria threw her pyjamas onto the white tiled floor. Still wearing the vomit splattered gold top and mini skirt, she took a step towards Joanna. Her head pounding so hard it made her ears throb.

"Get out of there!" Gloria shrieked.

Joanna intimidated her; in truth, the woman frightened her, but those feelings were drowned by anger. Anger at Joanna for touching what had been her parents' bathroom. Anger at herself for allowing Rhetty and Joanna to manipulate her into this situation.

She clenched her fist and resisted the urge to pound Joanna on the head. *Watch your step, Gloria,* her mother's voice warned.

Joanna closed the cupboard and stood. She moved with exaggerated slowness.

"You're not a very good hostess, Gloria." She leaned one hand on the sink and placed the other on her hip. "I was just looking for toilet paper."

"I don't believe you. And I don't have to be a good anything." Gloria shook with outrage. "You're *not* my guest. I don't want you in my house."

"Calm down." Joanna held her hands out palms up in a placating gesture. "You're coming down, it's making you irritable. You need to take it easy." The last words came out as a warning.

Gloria's face felt hot. Joanna's condescending tone only added to her fury.

"What did you give me? You knew it would make me …" She searched for words. "It would make me *do* things."

Joanna laughed. "Make you act like an idiot? Is that what you mean?" She shrugged. "You didn't need any help from me, you do that all by yourself."

Gloria took another step towards her. She narrowed her eyes. "You know those guys, don't you?"

"What guys?"

"You told them to do that to me." It had been at the back of Gloria's mind all evening. She'd seen Joanna talking to the two men when she first entered the bar. She gave Gloria the pills. She told Smiley when to strike. Now the accusation was out, Gloria had no doubts about its veracity.

"Do what?" Joanna asked frowning. If Gloria didn't know better, she would have believed that Joanna was genuinely confused.

"You're a drug dealer. I should phone the police and have you —"

Joanna moved with unexpected speed. She grabbed Gloria by the face, squeezing her cheeks between her thumb and fingers. Her other hand wrapped around Gloria's throat. She spun Gloria around and pushed her back against the sinks.

Gloria felt her head hit the mirror and her back smack against the marble vanity. She tried to twist her face out of Joanna's grasp, but the woman's fingers only squeezed harder.

"Listen to what I'm telling you," Joanna hissed, her face centimetres from Gloria's. "You call the police and I'll beat that pretty face of yours to a pulp. By the time they get here, you'll be so messed up that all the king's horses and all the king's men will never put Gloria together again."

Joanna's fingers dug into the soft flesh on Gloria's throat. The fingers on her other hand mashed Gloria's cheeks against her teeth. With each threat, Joanna shook

Gloria's face from side to side. The pressure on her throat made it impossible to swallow. She tried to hold the tears back, but the shock of the attack and the pain that came with it sent tears coursing down her cheeks.

"You make me sick. You've never had to work for anything in your miserable private-school-girl life."

Pinned against the vanity, unable to breathe or speak, Gloria clawed at Joanna's hands. She dug her nails into the back of the woman's left hand and raked the skin.

"Fuck," Joanna cursed but didn't release her grip. If anything, the pressure on Gloria's throat intensified.

Joanna leaned in closer and sniffed. "God, you stink." She wrinkled her nose in disgust.

Gloria let go of Joanna's hands and felt around on the vanity searching blindly for anything she could use to make the woman stop. Her vision blurred; her lungs screamed for air. She needed to force Joanna to let go before she passed out.

"Nod, if you understand what I'm telling you," Joanna asked pleasantly, as if talking to a child.

Gloria's hand found her father's antique shaving mirror. The base was marble. She wrapped her fingers around the stand and swung it upwards. The base connected with Joanna's cheek and made a cracking sound.

Joanna shrieked and let go of Gloria. She stepped back with her hand to her face.

"You fucking bitch. I think you broke my cheekbone." Her voice sounded strange, as if the top part of her mouth wasn't moving properly.

Gloria coughed and gulped air. Her throat burned with every breath. Still clutching the mirror, she slid sideways trying to put some distance between her and Joanna.

Joanna dropped her hand and Gloria could see the swelling already ballooning on the woman's face. Gloria's eyes slid past Joanna to the door. She needed to get out of the bathroom and get to Rhetty. Get to the phone. Her legs threatened to fold under her.

As if reading her thoughts, Joanna stepped between her and the door.

"You're not leaving," she said through gritted teeth and lunged forward.

Without thinking, Gloria swung the mirror. This time she thrust from the shoulder and put as much force into the swing as she could muster. As Joanna charged, the base of the mirror connected with her forehead. A sickening "thwack" resounded, and a line of blood appeared across the woman's skin. Joanna stopped moving and stood there. Her eyes looked large and round. She blinked a few times and then blood ran down her forehead filling her eyes.

Gloria watched as a flap of flesh opened up along Joanna's forehead. It looked like a huge, red mouth. Joanna blinked a few more times sending droplets of blood splashing in red arcs across the vanity. Her mouth opened and a "humph" of air rushed out. Then her legs buckled – like a puppet with the strings suddenly cut.

Joanna landed hard in a sitting position, legs bowed out on each side. She swayed and then fell back. Her head smacked the tiles.

Gloria felt a tremor begin in her knees. It travelled up her body gathering momentum until her whole being shuddered. She dropped the mirror, unaware of it hitting the floor and shattering. She took a step towards Joanna and called her name. The word came out as little more than a husky sob.

Joanna's eyes were open. For a split second, Gloria thought it meant she was conscious. Then she realised they were awash with blood and stared fixedly at the ceiling. The flap of flesh hung down over the woman's eyebrows, revealing something white and shiny underneath. It took a second for her to react to what she was seeing.

Joanna's skull.

Gloria whimpered and stumbled back. She had to get out of the room. If she stared at Joanna any longer she'd start to scream and never stop.

She turned on rubbery legs and grasped the door handle. The next thing she knew, her feet were pounding down the hall. When she reached the kitchen, she turned right and skidded into the room.

"Rhetty!" She forced the word out of her injured throat.

Open bottles and empty ice trays littered the sink, but otherwise there was no sign of her. Her mind refused to work, all she could think of was the shiny white patch on Joanna's forehead. Gloria grabbed the counter top to steady herself. She closed her eyes and tried to get her breathing under control. *Rhetty will know what to do.*

Her throat burned and her head felt too heavy for her shoulders. She stumbled towards the sink and turned on the tap. She put her mouth to the water and gulped, letting the cold water sooth some of the pain. She leaned forward and let the water wash over her face. The icy shock got her moving.

She turned and sprinted through the hall and into the main room. The French doors were open and the white gauzy curtains that framed them, floated on the breeze. She could see the lights on outside. Gloria stopped and laced her hands on top of her head. She hesitated.

Is Joanna dead?

The question repeated over and over in her mind: *Is she dead? Is she dead? Is she dead?* She thought of the woman's eyes, open and filled with blood – the gash on her forehead. Gloria had little doubt she'd killed her.

Panic propelled her forward. She hurried outside and found the deck as empty as the kitchen. Then she noticed the tray on the table. Three glasses, a bowl of ice, and a jug of something pink and fizzy.

"Rhetty?" She called as loudly as her injured throat would allow.

"I'm down here." The response came from the garden below the deck.

Gloria felt a moment's relief. She was nine-years old again with Rhetty, her saviour. *Rhetty will know what to do, she always knows what to do.* Gloria stumbled to the steps and looked down. Silver moonlight lit up the garden.

"It looks like a meteor hit your back yard." Rhetty gestured to the enormous crater that engulfed the area below the stairs. She stood next to a huge yellow excavator that crouched like an iron giant in the dark. "I can't wait to see what it looks like when the pool goes in." She smiled up at Gloria.

Gloria heard the words, but their meaning was lost on her. She put her hands against her temples and squeezed.

"Rhetty. Rhetty, please. I…" She didn't know how to finish or what to say, so instead, she stood at the top of the stairs and sobbed.

The smile fell away from Rhetty's face. She scrambled forward, taking the steps two at a time. She drew Gloria into her arms and stroked her hair.

"What's wrong? What's the matter?"

Rhetty's arms felt strong and steady around Gloria's back as her life-long friend guided Gloria's head down onto her shoulder. Her fingers brushed the welts already turning into bruises on the back of her neck. Gloria winced and drew back.

"It's okay. I'm here," Rhetty murmured, just as she'd done seven years earlier when Gloria woke from her coma, and learned of her father's death. Gloria had been driving and lost control.

She wanted to stay safely cocooned in Rhetty's arms, but this time there were no words to soothe the guilt. She pulled back and held Rhetty at arm's length.

"It's Joanna." She wiped her eyes with the back of her hand. "I think … I think she's dead." The last word stuck in her throat.

Rhetty shook her head and gave a weak laugh. "What are you talking about?" She seemed about to say more, but stopped.

Gloria let go of her friend's shoulders and looked into her eyes. The moonlight reflected there. It looked dark, like a candle at the bottom of a deep well.

"Where is she?" Rhetty asked flatly, her face stolid.

"The bathroom. She –"

Before she had finished, Rhetty pushed past her and darted into the house. Gloria followed, hurrying to keep up.

"I didn't mean to do it. She attacked me and it all just happened. I couldn't breathe. I just wanted her to let go." Gloria knew she was babbling, but she couldn't stop. She had to make Rhetty understand, but the words came out wrong.

Rhetty didn't turn or acknowledge Gloria's clumsy explanation. She strode through the house, her heels clicking on the floor. She reached the bathroom and stopped. The door stood ajar. A bar of light fell across the stone floor of the hallway. Gloria's hand hovered around her injured throat as she watched Rhetty push the door open and step inside.

Gloria didn't follow, instead she leaned her back against the wall and slid down until she sat crouched on the floor. She circled her arms around her knees and waited. She heard Rhetty's heels on the tiles, then rustling. *Was she checking Joanna's pulse?* She closed her eyes and prayed the woman's heart was still beating. Then they'd call an ambulance and this nightmare would be over.

Gloria heard movement and looked up. Rhetty stood over her, arms hanging at her sides, her face partially concealed by shadows.

"She's dead." She ignored Gloria and walked back towards the kitchen.

Chapter Thirteen

March 4th 2015

Gloria pushed the bathroom door open, her heart hammering in her throat. She didn't want to enter the darkened room, so she curled her hand around the door frame and used her fingers to find the light. She flicked the switch. The image of Joanna – pools of blood filling her eyes and her glistening skull – flashed through Gloria's mind. The image vanished as stark white light flooded the room.

The double sinks and marble vanity gleamed in the light. The white tiled floor remained spotless. At the far end of the room, the shower and bathtub looked dry and unused. The lid was down on the toilet. A sharp odour of bleach filled the air. Nothing indicated that Rhetty had been in there. Gloria shook her head and turned off the light.

She stood in the hallway and ran her hand through her hair. If Rhetty *was* missing, she should contact someone. She quickly dismissed the idea as ludicrous – it had been less than twenty minutes since Rhetty sat on the deck. There were dozens of explanations for her sudden disappearance. She might have gone for a walk.

In the dark?

The answer suddenly hit her. Her phone. It was in her bag. All she had to do was call Rhetty. Such a simple idea, she wondered why she hadn't thought of it sooner. She headed back towards the main entrance. After twenty minutes running around in a panic, it felt good to have something solid to hold on to.

She grabbed her bag off the hall table and flipped it open. She always kept her phone in the little pouch just under the clasp. She reached in and grabbed it. The screen looked filthy. Gloria frowned and held it up to the hall light. She was about to turn it over when a damp woody stench stung her nostrils. Gritty earth smeared her fingers.

Gloria turned the phone over and grimaced as the crazy cartoon face laughed back at her. She dropped the phone and backed up the hall. She felt lightheaded and braced herself, putting her palm flat against the wall. A riot of questions filled her head, all clambering for answers. The most frightening: *am I going mad?*

Gloria pushed off the wall and pressed the balls of her hands against her temples. She didn't believe in ghosts so there had to be a logical answer. *Was all this Rhetty's doing?* Rhetty had suggested the Easy Eight bar. She'd shown Gloria the phone. *She* had insisted they drive to Herron. The more Gloria thought about it the less far-fetched it seemed. But that led to the question, *why?* Why would her oldest and dearest friend torture her this way? And why wait four years to do it?

The rush of adrenalin she'd been running on dissipated, leaving her muscles weak and her head pounding. She needed to calm down and think. Gloria sat down on the floor. The stone felt cold against her butt and thighs. She closed her eyes and took a deep breath, then let it out slowly. She repeated the process five times, resisting the urge to jump up and pace around fretting.

When she opened her eyes, the light-headedness had passed and the pounding in her head lessened. She caught sight of Joanna's phone lying on the floor a few metres away. *Check your journal.* For some reason, staring at the laughing cartoon made her think of the message on the whiteboard.

When Rhetty asked her about her journal, she'd lied. *Why?* Was there something about Rhetty she needed to remember? All day, she'd been focused on Joanna and not really thinking about what was right in front of her.

Gloria stood up cautiously, not wanting to set off another wave of dizziness. She went to the kitchen first and re-read the message.

Check your journal.

She tapped her index finger on the whiteboard and tried to remember writing the reminder. She shook her head in frustration and headed for the bedroom.

Gloria turned on the overhead light. During the day, the view from this room was a spectacular panorama of virgin bush and glimpses of the estuary. Now with darkness blanketing the house, the window was a large black mirror beyond which anything could be lurking. Gloria stared at her reflection in the glass and wrapped her arms around herself, rubbing her hands up and down her bare arms. The thought of someone standing unseen on the other side of the window made her shiver. She pulled the white silk curtains closed.

A nineteenth century pale blue armoire stood against the wall opposite the bed. She kept her journals on the top shelf. There were ten journals tied together in bundles of five, each bundle secured with yellow silk ribbon tied in a big loopy bow. One journal sat on top of the pile, when completed, it too would be added to a bundle. Gloria stood on her toes and retrieved the book.

She ran her fingers over the soft leather cover. The feel of the book brought back memories. After her accident, the surgeon – a man with thinning ginger hair and erudite green eyes – suggested she keep a journal. He said that recording her thoughts, memories, and even mundane daily events would help her with her short and long-term memory. At first Gloria used a simple spiral notebook, but after the first year, she found an online site that supplied beautifully crafted journals. The covers were soft brown leather and the pages rich, unlined Khadda paper made from recycled cotton, left over from the massive garment trade in India. Gloria loved the luxurious otherworldly feel of the books.

She took the journal and sat on the bed just as she'd done a thousand times. The familiar aroma of leather and fresh cotton filled her nostrils, and with it came memories. Not clearly formed, but glimpses; foretastes of what she would find when she opened the book. *Do you really want to remember?* It was a whisper, a soft lilting voice in her mind. For a moment, Gloria considered putting the journal away and driving back to Perth.

She sat on the bed, her feet resting on the cheerful blue and cream rug her mother had carefully chosen and lovingly placed. Everything in the house had been placed here because her mother wanted the Herron house to be a home. A safe and beautiful place where her family could laugh and relax.

Gloria's hands trembled. Her mother had always been gentle, but strong. She'd fought the cancer until there was little left of her. Gloria needed to find some of that strength. Whatever was in the journal, she would face it.

She flipped open the cover and skimmed through the first few pages. She remembered writing about her visits to Dr. Chambers, her therapist, or Chris, as he preferred to be called. He recommended she increase her medication and consider intensive therapy. Mention of a shopping trip to Melbourne and an encounter with a man she met online. *An empty lonely life.*

She read on, not sure what she expected to find. *You know what you'll find,* the voice warned. She ignored the whisper in her head and continued. The next entry, in February, was little more than a few lines.

> *I've decided to stop taking the medication. It makes me feel numb – and hungry. I know Dr. Chambers is against it, but I'm tired of only half-feeling things. I want to be myself before I forget who I was. Crazy!*
> *Anyway, if my memory gets worse or I have blackouts, I can always go back on the pills. There are things I want so badly to forget.*

Gloria stopped reading and rubbed the corners of her eyes. She remembered making the decision to stop her medication and sure enough, her memory had worsened. At first it had been small things like appointments and getting days mixed up. Then she started to forget whole days. Not exactly blackouts, but missing time. Until now, she hadn't really acknowledged the extent of the problem. *But how did any of this involve Rhetty?*

She turned the page and noticed that her handwriting changed. While still clearly hers, it looked scratchy and rushed.

She read.

With each sentence her heart beat faster. Her eyes skittered across the page and her mouth opened and closed in silent panic. When she reached the end of the last entry, she let go of the journal and stared blindly ahead. The book slipped from her lap and bounced on the rug.

Chapter Fourteen

March 6th 2011

The tears had dried up, but Gloria remained on the floor. She'd heard nothing from Rhetty since she'd come out of the bathroom and announced Joanna's death. Gloria wondered if she'd called the police yet. She checked her watch. *After midnight.* She tried to imagine what it would be like to be handcuffed and taken away. *Would it matter that she had acted in self-defence?* She didn't think so. She'd killed someone.

She could feel the panic crawl its way up her throat. She balled up her fist and pushed it into her mouth. She had no doubt she would go to prison. They would do blood tests and find out that she'd taken drugs. She'd be the spoilt rich girl who got high and went on a murderous rampage. Her lungs felt tight, she needed air.

She struggled to her feet on rubbery legs and walked towards the kitchen. If she could talk to Rhetty, explain what happened, then maybe they could find a way out of this together. *Help me hide the body?* That's what Gloria really wanted. *No.* She corrected herself, she really wanted to turn back time and undo the ugly thing she'd done. But that was impossible and it didn't matter how much remorse she felt, nothing could bring Joanna back.

She found Rhetty on the deck staring out into the night. She must've heard Gloria approach because she spoke without turning around.

"After you woke from the coma, you changed."

The comment took Gloria by surprise. She'd been expecting anger, tears, maybe even threats, but not this. She searched for something to say but her mouth felt dry and her mind whirled in overdrive.

"You were different." Rhetty sighed. "Needy, easily confused. Drifting from thing to thing –"

"Rhetty, there's no time for this now. I need your help." Gloria paused and tried to get her panic under control. "I... I don't want to go to prison."

"Of course I'll help you," Rhetty said still facing away from Gloria. "Let's have a drink first," she said and turned around.

Gloria had expected tears, but Rhetty's eyes were dry, her expression unreadable. Gloria followed her into the house and through to the kitchen.

"I think the situation calls for whiskey, don't you?" Her tone of voice made it sound like they were deciding what to order at a restaurant. "Will you get the ice? I left it on the deck."

Gloria opened her mouth to object. She didn't understand how Rhetty, who couldn't watch a scary movie, could be so calm. She wondered if her friend was in shock and the cool veneer would crumble at any minute. If so, Gloria didn't want to start an argument.

"Okay," she said.

When Gloria returned carrying the bowl of partially melted ice, Rhetty had placed two half-filled tumblers on the island bench. Next to the glasses stood an open bottle of whiskey. Gloria didn't remember having whiskey in the house. As if she'd read her mind, Rhetty said, "I bought the bottle when I stopped at the liquor store."

Gloria nodded and put the bowl of ice on the bench. Her hands felt numb from holding the bowl. She rubbed them together absentmindedly as she watched Rhetty drop handfuls of ice in each glass. Unlike Gloria's, Rhetty's hands were steady as a rock.

"Here you go," Rhetty said and handed Gloria a tumbler.

Gloria took the glass. The ice clinked as she lifted it to her lips.

"That will steady your nerves," Rhetty said, and took a generous sip of her drink. "God, what a night you've had. First Smiley and now Joanna."

The hairs on the back of Gloria's neck stood on end and a cold breeze brushed the back of her legs. She forced herself to swallow the whiskey in her mouth. It burned her already sore throat and soured in her stomach. Gloria licked her lips and put her glass on the island. The silence between them stretched. *Watch your step, Gloria.*

Gloria didn't know how Rhetty knew the guy's name, but the small changes in her friend's demeanour alarmed her almost as much as the mention of it. There was a stillness in the way she held herself that Gloria had never seen before. Her eyes, usually wide and concerned, were hooded and empty of any emotion. And suddenly the idea that Gloria might be in danger, crept into her mind.

She considered asking Rhetty how she knew about Smiley. The words were already forming in her mouth, but died on her lips. All night she'd had the feeling of being manipulated. That danger had circled her like a shark, but she'd been too stoned and too blind to see the one doing the manipulating.

Not Joanna.

Rhetty.

Gloria swallowed a second time and grimaced. She nodded towards the whiskey. "I needed that."

"Then why don't you finish it?" Rhetty said softly.

Gloria dragged her gaze from Rhetty and regarded the glass. The amber liquid looked cloudy. She frowned as a surge of wooziness swept over her.

"I don't feel well." Gloria tried not to let the fear show. She did feel strange, heavy-limbed and drowsy. But she also needed an excuse, a reason to get out of the kitchen. She tried to remember where she'd left her bag. If she could get to her phone... her thoughts trailed off. *Then what?* She couldn't call the police, not with Joanna lying dead on her bathroom floor.

"Let's go back to the bathroom," Rhetty said, and turned towards the sink.

In the second it took Rhetty to put her glass in the sink, Gloria made the decision to run. She rounded the corner and scrambled for the main room. She could hear Rhetty's heels clicking behind her. Gloria's legs were longer and she had bare feet, but the heaviness in her limbs made her slow and clumsy. Grateful that the French doors were open, Gloria bolted from the house.

She made a bee-line for the steps, crashing through the table and sending the jug of cocktails and glasses plummeting to the deck. Broken glass scattered before her, but Gloria moved too fast to avoid the carpet of shards. Glass crunched under her left heel. A searing poker of agony shot through her foot.

She faltered and almost fell to her knees. But a quick glance over her shoulder was enough to propel her forward. Rhetty barrelled towards her, her mouth drawn back in a savage grimace as she held aloft a red-handled carving knife. *That's my mum's knife,* Gloria thought stupidly and scampered down the steps.

When she reached the second step from the bottom, Gloria leapt onto the lawn. Her bloodied heel hit the wet grass and slid out from under her. She landed on her backside with her right knee bent painfully under her. She yelped in pain and rolled sideways.

Rhetty hit the grass and then cursed. Gloria risked a backward glance and watched Rhetty struggle to remove a heel stuck in the lawn. It gave her enough time to clamber to her feet and move.

Her breathing came in short gasps and her knee throbbed with every step. She had no idea where she was going. She skirted around the dark hollow gouged out of the lawn. The hole where the pool would be sunk looked like an abyss, black and bottomless.

She could hear Rhetty's laboured breathing and her feet thumping on the grass. Gloria's eyes darted in every direction looking for something, anything that she could use to stop Rhetty from plunging that knife into her flesh. She headed towards the excavator and spotted a glint of light. A piece of metal, capturing a beam of moonlight, winked at her.

As Gloria approached, she whispered a prayer of thanks to the workmen installing the pool and snatched up the shovel. She spun around waving the head of the shovel in front of her. Rhetty slowed, but kept moving forward.

"Stop!" Gloria gasped. Her lungs burned and her arms felt so heavy, she could barely hold the shovel. "Rhetty, *please* stop." She swung the shovel back and forth in front of her.

Rhetty held the knife loosely at her side. She stopped moving, but seemed unfazed by the shovel. "Put that down and come inside. You're just making this more difficult." Her tone sounded calm, conversational.

Gloria laughed humourlessly and inched backwards. "*You're* chasing me with a knife for Christ's sake and I'm the one making things difficult?" Gloria shook her head at the absurdity. Rhetty had stood by her during the worst moments of her life. They were closer than sisters, because sisters argued and bickered but they never did.

"Is this because of what I did to Joanna?"

"No, it's not because of her. Though I have to say, I'm impressed. I didn't think you had it in you. I guess you showed her." Rhetty paused, and then took a sudden step forward. "Bam!" She sang and clapped the fist holding the knife into the open palm of her other hand.

Gloria flinched, the shovel almost slipped out of her grasp. "Please, Rhetty," she begged. "This isn't you. This doesn't make any sense. We're friends." Gloria's eyes blurred and she felt tears on her cheeks.

"Friends? All I am to you is a reflection of your needs." She took another step forward. "Friend, sister, mother. Whatever Gloria *needs* —"

"No. Rhetty, I … I love you. Why are you doing this?"

"Money." The light of the moon lit up Rhetty's face revealing cold, pitiless eyes, and a downturned mouth. "After your father died I went with you to his solicitor." She paused. "Oh, what was his name again?"

"Alan Luckman," Gloria said softly. It occurred to her that she was finally seeing the *real* Rhetty. The face she kept hidden: cold, cruel and remorseless. In that moment, Gloria realised there would only be one way out of this nightmare.

Rhetty nodded and moved within centimetres of the shovel.

"Yes, that's it. I'll need to contact him." She gestured towards Gloria. "When this is all over, that is. Anyway, I went with you because you needed me to support you. You do remember all this, don't you?"

Gloria nodded. She tried to focus her mind on keeping the shovel up in front of her, but her fingers grew numb.

"When he told you how much your father was worth, you just nodded." Rhetty shook her head. "Here you are being told you'd just inherited millions, and you were too busy playing the wounded princess to care." Rhetty's eyes were wide and bits of spit flew from her lips. "But then, then you told him you wanted him to draw up a will leaving everything to me." She used the tip of the knife to point at her own chest. "Well, all I had to do then was wait. For the right time." She opened her arms and gestured to the house. "Tonight's the night."

"You can't just kill me, they'll put you in prison. You'll never see a cent."

Rhetty nodded. "You *were* going to accidently drown when we were having our late-night estuary swim, but –" She shrugged. "That all changed when you killed Joanna. Now it's going to look like you killed her when she was stabbing you." Rhetty made a stabbing motion with the knife.

Gloria's eyes followed the movement of the knife. The muscles in her back shrieked with the strain of keeping her arms out. A tremor slithered its way up her wrists.

"That shovel must be getting heavy," Rhetty whispered. "It'll be much easier if you just put it down." Her voice changed and became softer, more like the old Rhetty. "Come on. Let's go inside. You can finish your drink."

Gloria tried to ignore the coaxing voice and focus on the knife. She considered swinging the shovel and trying to hit the knife out of Rhetty's hand. But if she wasn't quick enough, Rhetty might charge her while she pulled back to swing.

"You've never forgiven yourself for killing your father, have you? Your head is so messed up, it must be a fight just to get through the days. After what those guys did to you tonight." She shook her head sadly. "You should be thanking me for having the courage to do what you can't."

"Did you?" Gloria's voice trembled. "Did you tell them to do that to me?" Rhetty tilted her head to the side and smiled. It was a sly gesture that sent an icy finger down Gloria's spine.

"I bet you didn't feel so rich and glamorous by the time Smiley finished with you."

Gloria's shoulders sagged under the weight of the betrayal. She could feel the fight drain from her body. Part of her wanted to stop this and go back into the house with Rhetty. She felt her arms lowering the shovel as if her body had made the decision for her.

Rhetty nodded. "That's right. We'll have a drink and you can rest." Her voice had taken on the soothing quality she always used when Gloria needed a shoulder to cry on.

The tip of the shovel touched the grass and a sob escaped Gloria's lips. Rhetty kept nodding and took a step closer, now only a meter and a half away. She had the knife at her side, but as she took another step, she raised it and held it in front of her. It was the move Gloria counted on.

She turned the shovel sideways and used both hands to swing the sharp edge. It slammed into Rhetty's fist. She screamed and stumbled. Gloria didn't wait to see if she'd dropped the knife. She lifted the shovel up past her shoulder and swung like she was hitting a baseball.

The broad flat base of the tool hit Rhetty across the shoulders and sent her staggering to her knees.

"I'm not so glamorous now either, am I!" Gloria bellowed, and lifted the shovel over Rhetty's head.

"Please, don't," Rhetty begged looking up at her, eyes wide with fear.

Gloria hesitated, the shovel still poised to strike. Her heart battered against her ribs and she could hear blood pumping in her ears. For a second, she felt the cold porcelain of the sink against her cheek and smelled the stench of the damp, rotten drain. Rhetty had sent those men. Gloria *wanted* to hit her. She wanted her to feel pain.

"Gloria, don't hit me, please." Rhetty's voice sounded small and frightened.

Gloria puffed out a breath and blinked. She could feel something wet and she realised it was tears, running down her cheeks and dripping onto her chest. She'd already killed one woman tonight, could she bring herself to do it again? If she did, she knew she'd be lost. The guilt would never let her go.

"I'm going inside to call the police," she said around harsh breaths. "Don't get up or I swear, I'll kill you." Her voice was flat. There was no feeling left in her.

Rhetty nodded and stayed on her knees. Gloria stared at her for a moment. She wanted to say more, but could think of nothing. Nothing that mattered now.

Gloria lowered the shovel and stepped away. She looked up and could see the lights on the deck. The house looked distant like a wavering tower. She forced herself to put one foot in front of another and move towards the light.

She'd taken three steps when she heard movement behind her. She turned in time to see Rhetty leap to her feet, knife in hand.

Gloria didn't hesitate. She turned her body and swung the shovel in one fluid movement. Time slowed, like the drip of a faucet when you're trying to sleep – *ahh, to sleep.*

Rhetty held the knife at her shoulder and lunged forward. Gloria took in the woman's bared teeth and wide eyes. She felt her shoulder strain as the heavy shovel flew around in a wide arc. At the last moment, Gloria turned the shovel so the side of the blade landed with a sickening crunch in the centre of Rhetty's head.

The base of the shovel sheared through skin and bone and created a fissure before lodging in place.

Time sped up dizzyingly.

Gloria howled and let go of the shovel's handle. Rhetty let out a guttural moan and crumpled. When she hit the ground, the base of the shovel slipped out of her skull and bounced once before coming to rest on the grass.

Gloria took a couple of hurried steps backwards before her bloody heel slipped out from under her and she fell. She didn't bother trying to get up, there was nowhere to go and nothing to run from. In the blackness of the surrounding bush, an owl hooted.

Chapter Fifteen

Gloria picked up the journal and placed it back in her lap. She didn't need to read the last entry again, the memories were back. Since stopping her medication, she'd made three trips to Herron with Rhetty. Only, Rhetty was dead and the trips, while real, were made alone. Rhetty meeting her at the Easy Eight, showing her the phone and driving with her to Herron were all a repeating fantasy Gloria's mind kept playing out. Gloria could see herself sitting alone in the Easy Eight while nursing two drinks, staring in a fugue-like state and occasionally mumbling to herself.

She closed the journal and ran her hands over the cover. That night, four years ago, became as clear now as if it were yesterday. She remembered burying Joanna and Rhetty in the excavated hole for the pool. It had taken her hours, using the same shovel she killed Rhetty with. The image of the two women's bodies lying tangled and bloody in the dirt hit her like a boulder. The weight of the knowledge hardened into a familiar burden, the loss and betrayal fresh and raw in her mind.

The room felt too bright. She bent over and slipped off her shoes, then leaned across the bed and flicked on the lamp. When she'd turned off the overhead light, she crawled into bed. Her body felt heavy, as if it were encased in ice and wanted to shut down. It took all her strength to reach out and turn off the lamp. She couldn't think anymore, she wanted the pain to stop. With the room blessedly dark, she closed her eyes and let sleep take her.

* * *

She woke to the sound of birds chirping and a bar of sunlight seeping through the crack in the curtains. Gloria sat up and threw back the covers. The journal lay on the far side of the bed. She glanced at it, but decided it would wait until she'd had her coffee.

She padded down the hall and made a quick detour to grab her handbag from the table. Picking it up, she noticed Joanna's phone still on the floor. She claimed it and headed for the kitchen. Yesterday the sight of the phone had repulsed and terrified her, but in the light of day, it was nothing more than a sad reminder of what human beings were capable of.

Ten minutes later, Gloria sat on the deck sipping her coffee. She looked past the pool and let her gaze rest on the estuary. The air seemed cooler than yesterday, and a slight breeze ruffled her hair. Last night she'd slept deeply and woke with a clear mind – and a plan of action. Making a decision and moving forward felt good. She felt lighter, more focused than she'd been in a long time.

Gloria noticed a kangaroo at the edge of the lawn, its long neck dipped down as it nibbled the damp grass. She smiled to herself and watched it graze. She felt a lonely sorrow, warm and heavy, settle on her shoulders. Not for Rhetty or Joanna, but for this beautiful place. After today, she didn't know when she would see it again.

She forced herself to keep the momentum she'd woken up with going. Reluctantly pulling her eyes away from the roo, Gloria stood. The sound of her movement startled the animal. It looked up at her with large, soft, brown eyes and regarded her for a moment. As if sensing she presented no threat, it bowed its neck and continued to work on the grass.

* * *

Gloria, dressed in jeans and a black T-shirt, grabbed Joanna's phone from the kitchen and a set of keys she kept in her bedside cabinet. She stuffed the keys and the phone in the front pocket of her jeans. She had an important call to make, but first, there was one more thing to check.

Taking care to disengage the lock, she closed the front door and turned left away from the driveway and into the bush. About ten metres from the house sat a large red hunk of rock almost as big as a fire hydrant. Next to the rock lay a cluster of fallen gumtree branches. They were ancient and washed pale grey by years of sunlight. Gloria bent and pulled the branches to the side, piling them on the red brick gravel near the house.

Nearly ten minutes later, she stood and arched her back. It was just after eight, but the temperature had already started to climb. A fine line of sweat built up across her forehead and upper lip. She wiped it away with the back of her hand and surveyed the area she'd cleared. With the branches out of the way, an overgrown dirt road became visible.

Gloria looked over her shoulder to make sure no one was watching her. She could see the front of the house, her car and the part of the driveway that led to the road. Satisfied that she was very much alone, she left the clearing and headed into the bush.

A carpet of fallen leaves, seedpods, and small branches covered the track. On either side of the trail, trees and shrubs grew tightly together. Gloria stayed in the centre of the dirt road to avoid scraping her skin on the spindly branches that reached out from either side. The only sounds were her running shoes crunching on twigs and leaves, and the occasional chirping of birds.

Walking at a brisk pace for almost five minutes, Gloria watched the workshop and storage shed come into view. The dark green steel structure remained partially hidden by a blanket of thick bush, leaving only the front visible from the track. Gloria looked up at the expanse of cloudless sky. She guessed the roof would be easily spotted from the air if anyone cared to look. But down on the ground was a different story.

There were two roller doors on the front. The interior was separated by a dividing wall. Gloria's father had the workshop designed so that he could use one side for storage and the other as a shop. A workshop on the left housed a collection of tools, kayaks, crab nets, and fishing gear, along with a five-metre aluminium fishing boat and trailer. Gloria hadn't been in the workshop in years, its contents a reminder of a long-lost time in her life.

She stepped up to the roller door on the right. The concrete slab the building sat on was a patchwork of fine cracks. She reached into her pocket and pulled out the keys. Each of the roller doors was secured with heavy brass padlocks fastened to metal loops embedded in the concrete. Gloria crouched down and slid the key into the padlock and turned it.

For a second, the lock refused to move. Gloria dropped onto her knees, cursed under her breath and tried again. This time the cylinder turned and the lock sprang open. She put the lock and the key on the cracked cement floor. Wiping her sweaty hands on the front of her jeans, she grasped the bottom of the door and pulled. The runners on the side groaned and rattled and then the door slid up.

Gloria raised the door a metre or so and then stood so she could push it up over her head.

Sunlight penetrated the darkened space revealing the shrouded hulk that dominated the floor. She stepped into the storage shed. Tiny grains of dirt and sand skittered under her shoes. She let out a loud breath. Until this moment, a tiny part of her hoped the shed would be empty, and all her memories would prove to be yet another delusion.

She moved forward and grabbed the edge of the canvas tarpaulin. The air in the shed smelled faintly of petrol and mould. Gloria clenched her lips together and pulled. The large tarpaulin felt heavy with dust and the dirty stiffness that comes with age. It took both hands, but with a little wrangling she managed to wrestle it to the floor.

Clouds of fine dust filled the air. Gloria waved her hand in front of her face and sneezed. Rhetty's black Mazda sat on deflated tyres. A fine layer of dust settled on the bumper, but for the most part, the tarp had kept the car protected. Gloria reached out her hand and touched the back window. The glass felt cool under her fingers.

She walked farther into the shed, trailing her fingers along the car as if it would vanish if she broke contact with it. She wrapped her hand around the handle and pulled the driver's door open. It creaked in protest, but swung clear. The interior harboured shadows. The car's battery, long dead, offered no interior light. Gloria slid in and sat behind the wheel.

Rhetty's yellow jacket, the one she'd lent Gloria, lay on the passenger seat with Rhetty's handbag. She thought she caught a whiff of Voyage but it might've been her imagination. She pulled the phone out of her pocket and put it in the console between the seats. Placing her hands on the wheel, she leaned her head back. The last time she'd been in this car, she remembered only exhaustion. There'd been so many emotions that night, but in the end the exhaustion overwhelmed her like never before.

Chapter Sixteen

March 6ᵗʰ 2011

Gloria watched Rhetty's lifeless body for what seemed like hours. The night air had grown colder as the breeze picked up. Rhetty hadn't moved in a long time. When she first fell, her arms and legs twitched and she'd made a thick gurgling sound, like someone breathing through a snorkel. But now, everything was still.

Gloria didn't want to look at her friend anymore, but getting up meant going back into the house and facing Joanna's body. She looked up at the sky, a huge black expanse above her. She felt tiny and lost under its vastness. She wanted to lie back on the cool grass and stare at the stars.

I wonder how long it'll be before someone comes looking for me?
There is no one, remember.

She was truly alone now. She didn't have Rhetty anymore. *Did I ever have Rhetty?* The things that woman had done to her – had *tried* to do to her. She knew she should call the police. Every minute she waited made things look worse. *How much worse could it get?* She knew she would go to prison. Joanna and Rhetty had tried to kill her, but would anyone believe her? The police would talk to her doctors, they would find out that she had *problems*. They'd dig into her past. They'd know she'd been driving when her father was killed.

She ran her hands through her hair. She had to think. She looked around searching for an answer. Then it struck her. She clambered to her feet and walked closer to the pit. The pool would be put in the hole on Monday. She realised that if she buried Joanna and Rhetty in the hole, the pool would cover it, and their bodies would never be discovered.

Rhetty had told her that Joanna only had a mother who lived in Melbourne. Rhetty said the two despised each other and hadn't spoken in years. Gloria paced back and forth going over every angle. She thought about Rhetty's car and how easily it could be hidden. Joanna had left the bar before Gloria and Rhetty. No one knew they'd all gone to Herron together. That left just one problem... Malcolm.

She stopped pacing and headed for the house. She took the stairs to the deck two at a time, giving the broken glass a wide birth; bloody tracks from her injured foot led from the deck down the stairs. She realised her foot still bled. Not wanting to tramp blood through the house, Gloria pulled her top over her head and stood on one foot while she wrapped it around her wound. She wore no bra, the cool night air felt good on her naked skin.

She limped into the house and down to the bathroom. The door remained as Rhetty had left it, ajar. Gloria gave it a push and it swung open. She swallowed and straightened her back.

She kept her eyes averted as she opened the cabinet under the sink. She could smell something thick and metallic in the air. She realised it was blood. Her stomach lurched. She managed to lean over the sink just in time to vomit a stream of frothy water that hit the basin and splashed back against her cheeks. She dry-heaved a few more times before she managed to get her stomach under control.

Hands shaking, she leaned down and grabbed the first aid box and limped over to the toilet. She put the lid down and sat so that she could examine her heel. She peeled the material away and decided it wasn't too bad: a small gash, about four centimetres long. Her feet were filthy, covered in dirt and grass stains. She put a large band aid over the gash, deciding to worry about cleaning the wound later. Tossing the first aid box onto the vanity, she hurried out of the room.

Next, she found an old pair of trainers in the bottom of the armoire. Not wanting to get dirt on the bed, she sat on the floor and pulled them on. She realised she was still naked from the waist up. She considered finding a T-shirt but decided it would only be something else she'd have to dispose of later.

Her mind kept coming back to Malcolm. She left the bedroom and went in search of Rhetty's phone. In the kitchen, she found Rhetty's bag on the counter next to an open bottle of champagne. She opened the bag and rummaged through the contents. She found a packet of cigarettes and a plastic lighter. Gloria frowned and wondered when Rhetty had started smoking again. She almost laughed at her own stupidity. She still thought she knew Rhetty even after the woman tried to kill her.

Gloria fished the phone out of the handbag and swiped the screen. She opened the messages and found the top one from Malcolm. Gloria scrolled through and started reading. Her heart beat a little faster. Clearly, he was angry with Rhetty. The first message was from much earlier that night.

Malcolm: You were supposed to be here when I got home.
Rhetty: I'll see you tomorrow.
Malcolm: I'm not doing this anymore.
Rhetty: Up to you.
Malcolm: I want you to move out.
Malcolm: ?
Malcolm: Are you with her?

Gloria hesitated. Four words. A simple question, yet it clarified every suspicion she'd held about the nature of Rhetty and Joanna's relationship. She waited for the emotions to hit her. Surprise? Bitterness? But she wasn't surprised, she realised she'd always known and returned her attention to the screen.

Malcolm: I'm packing your stuff. Pick it up tomorrow or I'm dumping it in a charity bin.

The last message had been sent at around nine o'clock. Gloria checked her watch: almost one-thirty in the morning. She bit her bottom lip and stared at the screen. She typed a message and sent it before she could change her mind.

Rhetty: Do what you want. I won't be back.

Gloria grimaced. She wondered if Malcolm would take the message seriously or would he think it was just a drunken text? She didn't have to wait long. The phone beeped in her hand.

Malcolm: Fuck you, bitch.

Satisfied that she had at least bought herself some time before anyone came looking for Rhetty, Gloria's hand hovered over the power button. She knew it was pointless now, but she had to know if Rhetty had messaged Smiley. She went back to the messages and sure enough, she found something. A single one-word message.

S: Done.

The *received* notification read ten-fifteen. Right around the time Rhetty found her in the ladies' room. She supposed she should be angry, but instead she felt empty. She guessed she might be in shock and decided that was a good thing – at least she wouldn't have to feel anymore.

She checked Rhetty's recent calls and sure enough, Rhetty had called Joanna at 10:48.

She turned off the phone and took out the battery. She put the battery on the island bench. She would smash it and dispose of it later. Everything else, she shoved back into Rhetty's bag. Then she took a dustpan and brush and went out onto the deck and cleaned up the glass. When she returned to the kitchen, she dumped the glass in the bin in the pantry. She made a mental note to empty the bin into the wheelie outside before she left.

She checked the time, it was almost 2:00 am. *Sunday.* The pool men wouldn't arrive until Monday morning. She had the whole day to make sure everything was taken care of. Even so, she wanted to have the bodies buried before the sun came up. It seemed to be a task best suited to the cover of night.

She thought about the next step, the saliva in her mouth evaporated. She went to the cupboard over the sink, took out a glass, turned on the tap and filled it. Gloria drank the entire contents in three gulps, ignoring the drips that ran down her chin and splashed onto her bare chest.

Next, she went to the laundry and found some old dust sheets under the sink and a heavy-duty torch. In the long narrow cupboard opposite the sink, she pulled out a mop, bucket, and a length of nylon rope. Satisfied that she had everything she needed, she left the mop and bucket in the laundry, taking the sheets, torch and rope back to the bathroom.

* * *

Two hours later, Joanna and Rhetty's bodies lay in a large hole within an even larger hole. Their heads were wrapped in dust sheets, now stained with dirt and blood. The hole Gloria dug was about two metres deep and two metres wide. Although compacted and awaiting the layer of crushed gravel that would be added on Monday, the ground was surprisingly soft and easy to dig. The hardest part had been dragging Joanna out of the house and down the steps.

Gloria stood over the two women. She shone the torch around the hole. Rhetty lay on the bottom with

Joanna sprawled over the top of her, half her body on Rhetty and the other half in the hole. *No one could ever come between them, Joanna finally had what she wanted.* She wondered if she should say something, but she didn't believe in God so what was the point of praying?

"I'm sorry," she said aloud. "I didn't want any of this."

She put the torch down next to the hole, picked up the shovel and began filling the grave. Afterwards, she got on her hands and knees and tried to rake the earth over with her fingers. Soon realising the area was too large for her to settle by hand, Gloria sat back on her heels. She rubbed a gritty finger across her upper lip and scanned the pit for something she could use to flatten the ground. Just as the shovel had appeared when she needed it, now the orb of torch light found the bare steel of a compacting roller.

"Thank you," she said to the God she didn't believe in, and dug her hands into the earth to push herself up.

The roller was heavier than it looked, raw steel wrapped around concrete. The handle chest high, Gloria had to hunch her shoulders and push with her elbows skywards. Going down the slope towards the graves was fairly easy going. Apart from the area where she'd been digging, the pit had already been compacted, eliminating any bumps and burying any debris. She pushed forward and the barrel rolled over the grave.

Turning was where the problem started. The heavy concrete in the barrel made it difficult to manoeuvre. Gloria pushed forward and then pulled back, her hands burned with blisters from the earlier digging. After wasting at least ten minutes trying to turn the thing, Gloria realised that she would have to wheel the roller in a circle and come back around each time she made a pass over the grave. Her face almost blackened with grime, only the whites of her eyes visible, she worked the roller back and forth until satisfied that the ground looked flat.

Grabbing the torch, she checked the area; she didn't think anyone would notice the ground had been disturbed and it would have another day to settle before the workmen arrived.

She stepped around the area where the bodies were buried and made her way to the shallow end of the pit. She tossed the shovel up and out of the hole and then did the same with the torch. Grabbing the length of nylon rope that she'd tied to the excavator, her arms ached with the effort of climbing out after all the heavy lifting and digging. The rope slipped back through her blistered fingers and she slid down the side of the hole scraping her breasts and stomach against the loose earth. *I'm trapped*, she thought. *The three of us will be together forever.* A sound that was part laugh, part scream, burst out of her mouth.

She imagined herself caught in the pit like an animal. When the workmen arrived on Monday they would find her half naked and covered in dirt. They'd think she was mad and call the police. She looked around, the walls of the pit looked black. She couldn't stay down here, not with Joanna and Rhetty. She closed her eyes and saw two heads, still wrapped in bloody dust sheets pushing their way out of the earth. She tasted sand and grit on her tongue, and her mouth filled with saliva. *Just keep moving,* she told herself, trying to force back the panic that built inside her. She just needed to get the circulation in her hands moving and then she'd be able to pull herself up and out.

Gloria opened and closed her hands at least five times, then she rubbed them together. Rolling her shoulders back a few times, she shook her arms. Not only did the exercise get the blood moving, it also helped to calm her nerves. She stepped up to the rope, sucked in a deep breath and took hold. This time she used her toes and dug small foot holds in the side of the pit.

Gloria gritted her teeth and passed her left hand over her right, grasping the rope and then pushing up with her toes. When she was within reach of the top, she swung her right arm over the side and grasped the lawn. With one more push, she yanked the top half of her body out of the pit. She crawled forward and at the same time snaked her right leg up and over the side.

She lay on her stomach panting like a dog before rolling over onto her back. This time the night sky looked more welcoming. Gloria let out a deep sigh. With the hardest part done, all that remained was cleaning up and moving the car. When it was all over, she promised herself a hot shower, a strong cup of tea, and at least six hours of sleep.

* * *

Two hours later, Gloria had scrubbed the bathroom floor with bleach – she'd read somewhere it masks any trace of DNA. She'd also washed all the dishes and wiped any surfaces she thought Joanna might have touched – and she'd left more fingerprints in the house than any normal person would have. She wasn't worried about what Rhetty had touched because she'd been in the house many times, but as far as anyone knew, Joanna had never set foot in the place – and she intended to keep it that way.

Finally satisfied that everything was done, she kicked off the caked trainers and peeled off her black mini skirt and lace underpants. After hours of digging and cleaning, the skirt looked like little more than a filthy rag. *It would have been easier to work naked*, she thought absently. She stuffed the clothes and shoes in a large black garbage bag with the gold top she'd had around her foot. She thought for a moment and then removed her watch and tossed it in the bag. Gathering up the scrubbing brush and the rubber gloves, she put them in the bag. She'd put the bag in the boot of Rhetty's car before she moved it.

Pale light edged through the bathroom window. *It must be nearly 6:00 am.* She picked up the blue cotton pyjamas she'd thrown aside earlier and set them on top of the vanity. At the far end of the bathroom, near where Joanna had fallen, sat a free-standing bath with a shower overhead. The bath was surrounded by a white curtain hanging from an aluminium hoop. Gloria pulled the curtain back and turned on the shower.

As she stood waiting for the water to heat up, she caught sight of herself in the mirror over the sink and jumped. Her usually carefully tousled blonde hair clung to her head and hung around her shoulders in matted strings. Her face and upper body were streaked with dirt and blood, and her eyes were ringed with mascara. She looked like a savage. *Maybe that's what I've become?*

She turned away from her reflection and stepped over the bath and under the water. Gloria stood for a few minutes, just letting the hot water wash over her and massage her aching muscles. She looked at her feet and watched the brown water run over her toes and down the drain. When the water ran clear, she shampooed her hair.

Then she poured shower gel into her swollen left hand, afraid to use the sponge for fear she'd leave evidence behind. She washed her skin, rubbing gel over her face, shoulders and chest. It seemed that everywhere she touched, she discovered a scrape, bruise, or more swelling. Then she worked on her legs and lower body before repeating the process.

Finally, she put the plug in the bath and sat down. She let the water rise around her until it covered her shoulders. She sat forward and turned off the shower. The house fell into a sudden silence. Gloria lay back in the bath and thought about what she needed to do over the next few days.

She'd hide the car in the storage shed and then cover the dirt road with branches. When the workmen came on Monday, she'd hang around and make sure the pool was installed. At the end of the day, she'd ask one of the men to drop her at the train station. From there she'd be able to catch the train to the city and a taxi home.

She'd wait a week or so and then call Malcolm and ask if he'd heard from Rhetty. She'd let it slip that she'd lent Rhetty a large sum of money and wondered when she'd be back. Gloria nodded to herself as she went over the conversation in her mind. If ever questioned by the police, she'd tell them she had the money in her safety deposit box. Fortunately, she'd visited the bank and accessed the box only last week, so everything would check out. Malcolm would assume that Rhetty had skipped town with the money, but if he did go to the police, it would also explain why she hadn't used her credit card.

She thought about Rhetty's phone, she was tempted to keep it and check to see who tried to reach her, but decided it'd be too risky. She'd found Joanna's phone in her pocket. She recalled the feel of the woman's still warm body as she searched for the phone and grimaced. She'd have to take out the battery and smash it, but if she buried the phone somewhere near the storage shed, she could always dig it up and put a battery in later. That way she could keep tabs on who tried to contact the woman.

Gloria shivered, the water was almost cold. She stood up and pulled the plug. Her body felt heavy and her mind shut down. She decided to forget the tea and go straight to bed. When she woke up later, she'd have plenty of time to move the car.

She sat on the side of the tub and pulled on her pyjama bottoms, lifting each leg slowly like an arthritic old lady. She reached out to grab the pyjama top from the vanity and groaned. The muscles in her back and shoulder were seizing up. She struggled into the top and stood. Every movement set off an ache in either her legs, back, or arms. She turned off the light and shuffled slowly to the bedroom.

As she nestled her head into the feather pillow she couldn't help but wonder, *is it over or is this just the beginning?*

Chapter Seventeen

March 5th 2015

Gloria pulled the heavy tarpaulin over the Mazda and brushed her hands together to rid them of the fine particles of dust that clung to the canvas. The stuffy air in the storage shed clung to her like a heavy blanket. After today, she'd make sure that she'd never need to set eyes on that car again.

Gloria exited the shed and pulled down the roller door. Once it was locked, she turned and walked back the way she'd come. She moved briskly, drinking in the sunlight. Noticing the way that the sun glistened off the grass trees, she watched their swaying fronds turn from emerald-green to silver. A small degree of peace settled in her heart, the feeling as pleasant as it was surprising. She picked up her pace, eager to return to the house and be on her way.

* * *

Gloria made sure she turned off all the lights and locked the French doors. She thought of stepping out onto the deck for one last look, but decided she'd prefer to remember it as it had been earlier that morning with the kangaroo grazing on the lawn. She went to the kitchen and took her phone out of her bag.

It was time to make the call and move on with her life.

She scrolled through her contacts and found what she was looking for. Her hand hovered over the screen before she hit dial. She felt breathless as she listened. On the fourth ring a voice answered.

"Hi, Chris. It's Gloria. Gloria Kline."

"Hi, Gloria. I'm glad you called." His tone sounded relaxed and friendly. "You missed your last appointment. I was getting a bit concerned." He paused, waiting for her to fill the silence.

"Yes. Sorry. I … I've been thinking about what you suggested." Gloria bit her lip and opened up the cut. "You know, about intensive treatment."

"Has something happened?"

She wanted to tell him. She wanted to let it all out. She had killed two people and her mind buckled under the weight of the guilt.

"I … Yes."

"What is it? What happened?" His voice was calm and understanding.

"I stopped taking my medication and I sort of lost a bit of time." She stopped before she said too much.

He sighed on the other end of the line. It was a tired sound that made Gloria wonder how many sad desperate people he had to deal with every day.

"Alright, I want you to start back on your medication straight away. Do you have any left?"

"Yes. Yes, I've got half a bottle."

"Okay. Take one as soon as you get off the phone. And, if you're serious about taking your treatment further, I can arrange for you to enter a clinic." He paused and waited for her to answer. "Gloria?"

"Yes. Yes, I'm here. I want to do whatever it takes, but..." her voice trailed off.

"But what?" he asked softly.

"Not in Australia. I want to go away. Maybe America?"

"There are some excellent facilities here, but if that's what you want, I have a colleague in a private residential treatment facility in Colorado Springs. It's a highly regarded facility that's had great success treating patients experiencing psychiatric symptoms similar to the ones we've identified during your sessions." He paused and added, "It's expensive."

"The cost isn't an issue. Can you set up a referral?"

"Yes. I'll make some calls later today and have my receptionist contact you with the details."

Gloria opened her mouth to thank him, when he said something that surprised her.

"You've had a lot of sadness in your life, but none of it is your fault."

She could feel tears building in her eyes. She wanted to believe him. She knew she was broken, maybe even before everything that happened with Rhetty and Joanna. She didn't know if the treatment centre could fix her fractured mind, but for now, she'd settle for functioning well enough to lead a normal life.

"Thank you," she said trying to keep the tremor out of her voice.

After the call, Gloria took the bottle of pills out of her handbag and swallowed one with a handful of water from the tap. She tossed the bottle back in her bag and walked out of the house.

Epilogue: Ron and Linda

Linda Brackett hoisted the plastic washing basket onto her hip and slid the glass door open. The sound of the doorbell echoed through the house. Linda paused, one leg in the house and the other out. She looked over at her husband, Ron, hunched over the computer with his glasses perched on the end of his nose. She waited for him to look up.

"Ron?"

Ron dragged his eyes away from the screen. "Mmm?"

Linda let out a long sigh. "Can you answer the door? I have my hands full." She held the overflowing washing basket out in front of her.

"Alright. I'm going." He pushed his chair back from the kitchen table.

Linda stepped outside and put the basket back on her hip. She wanted to be able to see where she put her feet as she made her way along the path to the rotary clothes line. She glanced up at the clear sky and a slight breeze ruffled her hair. It was what Linda's mother would have called *a good drying day*.

She dropped the basket at her feet and grabbed a damp towel from the pile. As she straightened, she groaned and rubbed the small of her back. She pegged the towels in a line of four, corner to corner, as the smell of fabric softener filled her nose. Linda glanced over her shoulder. If Irene Fletcher had dropped by for another one of her surprise visits, Linda would let Ron listen to her go on and on about her grandson who could play the trumpet *and* the drums.

She began pegging another row of towels and smiled to herself, picturing Ron nodding politely as Irene leaned forward and whispered, "He's in the gifted and talented program, you know." Linda glanced over her shoulder again. Ron really was too kind-hearted, he didn't deserve to be subjected to a morning of Irene's nonsense.

Linda slid open the glass door, her eyes widening and her mouth dropping open. Ron was back at the table scratching his head and staring at the screen. He turned and caught the surprised look on his wife's face.

"So," he said with a chuckle. "You thought it was Irene and decided to save yourself by hiding in the back yard."

Linda dumped the basket on the table and planted a kiss on top of Ron's bald head. "Sorry, dal. I just couldn't face her again this week."

"Well you needn't have bothered hiding, it wasn't Irene," he said, trying not to look too pleased about the kiss. "It was Gloria Kline."

Linda walked over to the sink and began rinsing the breakfast dishes. "What did she want?"

Ron took off his glasses and pinched the bridge of his nose. "She said she planned on going away for a while." He frowned and stood up. "She seemed different, not so... not so spacey."

"What do you mean, not so spacey?" Linda asked, opening the door of the dishwasher.

Ron rubbed his chin. "Happier, like when she was a kid, you know?" He shrugged. "Before her parents..." His words trailed off.

Linda nodded. "That girl has had to deal with a lot of sorrow." She pulled out the top shelf from inside the dishwasher and put a cup and two bowls on the rack. "Maybe she's met someone."

"I hope so. She used to always have that chubby blonde girl with her, but I haven't seen her in..." He rubbed his chin again and looked out the sliding doors. "I don't know, but it must be a few years. I think that girl might've been her only friend."

Linda stopped stacking and put her hands on her hips. "That one was trouble."

Ron leaned his back against the draining board and crossed his arms. "Oh, Linda," he said with a laugh.

"Don't *Oh, Linda* me. That one had a swish in her tail and the devil in her eyes," Linda said, waving her finger at him.

"I don't even know what that means."

"It means," Linda said, pushing the top shelf in and bending to pull the bottom one out. "She's trouble."

Ron knew better than to argue with his wife once she'd made up her mind about someone. "Anyway, Gloria said she didn't know when she'd be back, but it wouldn't be for a long time. She said she'd make sure we got paid as usual and asked if we would cover the furniture with dust sheets."

"Dust sheets?" Linda stopped loading the dishwasher and frowned. "Now I remember she did have some dust sheets at the house, but I can't say I've seen them in a long time." She shook her head. "I wonder where they went?"

She made a mental note to have a dig around next time she was cleaning the place. Not that the thought of being in that house any longer than necessary appealed to her. The Kline house gave her the creeping shivers. The pool was nice and private, but Linda could never quite shake the feeling someone was watching her. All the weird notes Gloria wrote to herself didn't help matters either. If Linda wasn't so honest, she'd track down those journals Gloria kept telling herself to read and find out what all the fuss was about. But snooping wasn't her way. If, on the other hand, she found the journals while searching for the missing dust sheets, well that would be a different story.

"I asked her if she wanted me to drain the pool –"

"You did what?"

"Now now," Ron said, waving his hands in a calming gesture. "I had to ask, but she said no. She just wanted me to keep it clean and make sure the pump keeps working."

Linda let out a sigh and dropped a handful of forks into the cutlery caddy. She gave Ron a sideways smile. "You know how I love swimming in that pool. Besides," she said, rubbing her back. "It's good for my sciatic nerve pain."

Ron pushed himself off the draining board and walked around behind his wife. "And you know how much I like seeing you in your bathers," he said, and ran his hand over her sizable rump.

Linda chuckled as Ron rubbed his bristly chin against the side of her neck. "Maybe tomorrow I'll pack us a picnic lunch and we can spend the afternoon in the pool," Linda offered.

"I like the sound of that," Ron said with a smile.

BACKWOODS
MEDICINE

A prequel to Backwoods Ripper

ANNA WILLETT

Chapter One

Tommy pulled on faded jeans. Like every other garment in his pack, they needed a good wash. Last night he'd considered using the laundrette near the pub, but clean clothes cost money. He had fifteen dollars and eighty cents left in his wallet. The five bucks for the washer and dryer was an expense he'd have to do without.

Wishing he'd had the presence of mind to rinse out a T-shirt the night before, he sniffed the armpit of the cleanest-looking shirt he owned: a washed-out green *Jets* T-shirt that had seen much better days. Satisfied that it was close enough to clean, he pulled it over his head.

The ratty motel room reminded Tommy of the days he'd spent fronting Cataclysm. Touring around Victoria in a beat-up black van was an adventure when you were twenty-two, but at almost twenty-eight, the grimy room just made him realise his life was going nowhere.

Making as little noise as possible, he fished his phone out of his pack and shuffled into the bathroom. The air in the small space reeked of mould and, mingled with the unpleasant smell wafting up from the ancient pluming, the room reminded him of an overflowing garbage truck.

Grimacing, he flipped the toilet lid closed, sat, and reread Ralph's message.

Odin Records finally got back to me.
They love the demo. Meeting set for the 17th.
Get your ass back ASAP!

He'd read the message six times since last night and practically knew what it said word for word. Still, his heart kicked up a beat. He'd been waiting almost ten years for this. Odin Records was one of the biggest music producers in the world and he had a meeting with... well, he didn't know who exactly, but someone from the label was interested in him.

He drummed his fingers on his knee. Getting from Western Australia to Victoria in ten days wouldn't be too difficult; all he had to do was convince Tottie to drive him *and* put up with her for another week. He fired off a text: *I'll be there!!!*

Thinking about spending a week with the woman soured his good mood. When he met her four nights ago in Margaret River, she'd seemed okay. A little loud, but he was stoned at the time so he couldn't remember much beyond waking up next to her in the morning.

Tommy stood and turned on the tap, splashing cold water into his eyes. He'd been on a downward spiral since leaving Victoria, but all that had to change. He cleaned his teeth, washing away the taste of sleep and stale cigarettes. Time to cut back on the smoking. He combed his hair, grateful that he'd decided against shaving his head, a notion that seemed like a good idea when the group of surfies he'd been partying with all took the plunge. He almost did it too, but then a small part of him that refused to give up on his dreams remembered what Ralph, his sometimes agent, once told him. *You're selling the whole package, Tommy, not just the magic voice.* Tommy couldn't help smiling into the mirror.

"I hope you're right, Ralph." He spoke to the empty bathroom and immediately regretted it.

"Who you got in there?" Tottie's voice through the door was slurred. She was either half asleep or still half drunk.

She was still sprawled in bed when he opened the door. The thin, yellow sheet had slid down around her waist, revealing large pale breasts that hung over either side of her chest like deflated windsocks. Rather than being aroused by the sight of her half-naked body, Tommy felt a small wave of disgust. The sunlight peeking through the thin flowered curtains glinted off the stretch marks that carved jagged lines into her skin.

"I was just talking to myself, honey." He forced a smile that he usually saved for the stage. "We should get out of here and head east. You'll love Melbourne."

She scratched her armpit and rolled onto her side. "I'm hungry. Go get me a toasted sandwich." Her eyelids drooped. "I don't feel like driving anywhere." She yawned, revealing two black teeth in the back of her mouth.

"Okay, I'll be right back." Tommy watched her burrow her head into the pillow. He made himself count to five. "Damn, I'm skint. All right if I take the money out of your purse?" Tottie was a self-involved woman, but still he hated himself for leeching off her.

"Mm hm." His self-loathing turned into relief.

Tommy snatched up the plastic purse from the nightstand and flipped it open. The wad of cash took him by surprise. He had his suspicions about how she made her money, always disappearing to drop things off to *friends*. He guessed she was selling weed, maybe meth judging by the wad of cash. He shut the thoughts off, plucked out a twenty then slipped out the door.

* * *

Two hours later they were on the road. She took a bit of convincing, but eventually Tottie got on board with the idea of driving to Melbourne. Tommy guessed things were getting a bit hot for her in the southwest, because the more he talked about getting away from it all and making a new start, the more she relaxed.

"There's nothing but crap on the radio." She leaned over, pressing buttons, her stumpy fingers jabbing at the display. "God, I hate this country shit."

Tommy leaned his head against the backrest and closed his eyes. He'd skimmed ten dollars off the breakfast money by telling her he'd eaten his sandwich on the way back to the motel. He began to wonder if he could do the same thing later, maybe scrape enough together to buy a bit of juice for his phone. The last text had sapped his remaining credit; until he topped up, he could receive calls and texts but couldn't make any. His stomach growled. He snatched a sideways glance to see if she'd noticed, but she was still busy fiddling with the radio.

She glanced over and noticed him staring at her and smiled. Her over-bleached hair hung against her cheeks in limp clumps. In the four days they'd been together, he couldn't remember her washing her hair. He recalled her taking a shower that first morning, but since then he didn't think she'd washed. The idea of touching her made him want to scratch at his skin. *God, I must have been drunk for days.*

Tottie snapped off the radio. "Sing for me, sweetie?" She fluttered her lashes in a way that reminded him of someone having a stroke.

"My throat's a bit sore." He coughed into his hand.

"Oh, please?" She reached over and squeezed his thigh, her fingers sliding up the inside of his leg.

"Okay. Okay." He clamped his hand over hers and pushed her fingers away. "Don't distract me. I want to sing something nice for you."

She giggled and let go of his leg. *When did I become such a sleazy conman?* His mind tossed up Adeline's face. What would she think if she knew what he was doing? Suddenly he wanted to be out of the car, away from the smell of French fries and stale cola and the pile of burger wrappers that littered the floor. He wanted to be somewhere clean.

He opened his mouth to tell her to pull over and let him out, but all he could think of was the meeting with the exec from Odin Records. For years he'd worked the pub circuit singing covers for drunks who didn't care what he sounded like as long as the music was loud. God, how he wanted that record deal.

"Well?" Tottie poked him in the shoulder. "This trip's going to get old real fast if you don't start making an effort." She chuckled, but there was no mistaking the threat in her tone. She knew he was broke, *and* under the layers of sloppily applied eyeliner, she was as sharp as a butcher's favourite knife. Tottie knew he needed her, he could see it in the glint of her usually flat brown eyes. The look reminded him of a swooping bird, aggressive and predatory.

"Just getting my cords warm." He gave her a wink which did little to wipe away the hungry look in her beady eyes.

Tommy searched his repertoire for something upbeat and settled on *Call Me Maybe*. He'd never really liked the song, but he hoped it sent the right message.

Hey I just met you, the first words were a little flat, but Tottie didn't seem to notice, nodding her head and tapping her fingers on the steering wheel. By the time he was halfway through, a sinking feeling settled over him like a dirty blanket. He'd spent the last month partying, and when he needed money, busking. But standing on a street corner singing for disinterested shoppers never made him feel quite as pathetic as he did at that moment.

By the time he finished the song, tears had formed in his eyes, blurring the endless greenery as it flew by. His mind kept coming back to Adeline. He was a coward, walking out on her and disappearing for four months, all because she told him she was pregnant. How much lower could he get? *Judging by my last song, pretty low.*

"I'm going to close my eyes for a bit." He wasn't sleepy, but the thought of singing another song for the washed-up drug-dealing stripper made him want to block out the world.

Chapter Two

"Hey." Tommy felt something sharp jab into his ribs. "Wakeup. I need a sugar fix."

He must have nodded off, because he had absolutely no idea where he was. He didn't even notice the car stopping. Rubbing his eyes, he tried to focus on what Tottie was saying.

"I'm not your chauffeur." The shrill note in her voice told him she was about to go off on one of her rants.

Despite just waking from what must have been a deep sleep, the thought of listening to her berate him for the next five minutes made him feel exhausted. Ignoring her, he pressed the button to wind down the window. It was only when nothing happened that he realised the engine was turned off.

"Why am I the one doing all the driving? I'm the one that has to pay for everything and all you do is sleep."

Tommy opened the door, grateful for the blast of clean air. Tottie continued to screech at him while he leaned his head out and took a deep breath. They were in the parking lot of what looked like a roadhouse, a small rectangle of loose gravel fronting a rectangular brick building. There were two sad-looking benches on either side of the main door where a red sign welcomed travellers to the Million Miles Roadhouse.

Suddenly Tommy wished he were in Melbourne with its busy streets and rows of traffic. Something about the run-down roadhouse in the middle of nowhere really did make him feel like he was a million miles from home.

"Don't ignore me." Tottie grabbed his shoulder, digging her chubby fingers into his flesh. He tried to shrug her off but she held on. "Who the hell do you think you are?" She let go of his shoulder and gave him a slap on the forearm.

It wasn't a hard slap, barely enough force to leave a mark, but something about the sound of her palm striking his bare skin made Tommy's head buzz with anger. It was as if she'd poked a beehive that hung between his ears, setting a thousand winged-insects into motion. For the first time in his life, Tommy thought about hurting a woman. He wondered what it would be like to smash Tottie's piggy face into the steering wheel, imagining the satisfying crunch her nose would make as it hit the hardened plastic.

"Hey, asshole, I'm talking to you." She gave him another slap.

Tommy took hold of her hand. Moving with lightning speed, he gripped her fingers and pulled her hand down, pinning it to the seat.

"Keep your filthy hands off me." He spoke through gritted teeth, leaning back into the car so his face was close to hers. She flinched and blinked back tears. He felt a flicker of pleasure that was almost instantly swallowed by shame.

He let go of Tottie's hand, the surge of anger evaporating as quickly as it first exploded to life. As well as shame, he felt panic. He could see himself spending the next ten days replaying the moment over and over in his head as the chance of a lifetime slipped through his fingers.

"I'm sorry, honey. Please –" His next words were cut off by the sound of a rumbling engine and wheels hissing over the gravel. He looked over Tottie's shoulder to where an ancient Holden Ute bounced into the parking lot.

"Get out of my car." Tottie's voice was shaking.

"No, please, Tottie. Look, I didn't mean to hurt you. I just... You hit me and..." He trailed off, knowing he sounded like a pathetic schoolboy. He pulled his phone out of the pocket of his jeans. "Look, I've got to get to Melbourne. I've got a meeting with a record label and –"

She snatched the phone out of his hands and plunged it into a half-full paper cup of cola sitting in the console. The phone made a *plonk* as it landed in the flat liquid.

"I don't give a damn about your music shit. Take your guitar and get the hell out of my car." The tears had vanished. If he had hurt her, she was obviously over it. "You've got exactly three seconds before I start screaming." She puffed out her cheeks like an angry bull ready to charge.

Tommy glanced over her shoulder and saw a heavyset woman with grey hair climbing out of the Ute. He could imagine Tottie screaming and the woman racing over to help. Tottie telling the concerned stranger that he'd abused her, the whole thing ending in his arrest.

"Okay. Okay, I'm going." He grabbed his phone out of the cup and stepped out of the car.

He shoved the dripping phone into his back pocket and opened the rear door so he could grab his stuff. Not that he had much to his name – a small backpack and a guitar. Tottie barely gave him enough time to slide his things off the back seat before she turned on the engine. He watched her inch the car forward and swing it around in a sloppy U-turn.

She stopped alongside him and lowered the window. He took a half step forward, sure she'd changed her mind and was about to ask him to get back in the car. Instead, she held up the cup of flat cola and tossed it out the window.

The cup hit him in the chest, splashing tepid liquid over his T-shirt and neck. "Screw you. Loser." She spat the words at him through small, thick lips. He could see an angry red zit on the tip of her chin; it looked livid against her pale skin.

Before he could respond, she gunned the engine and took off, her parting shot completed by the spray of gravel that pelted his legs. Tommy lifted his T-shirt and looked at the dark-brown stain rapidly drying on the faded green fabric. He'd walked out on Adeline *and* his unborn baby. Not to set himself free, but so they'd have a better life. Even so, he guessed he got what he deserved.

He glanced over at the Ute and noticed a head through the back window of the cab. Not wanting whoever was in the vehicle to witness his further humiliation, he sniffed back tears and headed for the road. *When did I become such a cry baby?* The thought struck him as funny; if it weren't so tragic, he'd laugh.

Five minutes later, Tommy began to wonder if he was on a real road. Since walking away from the roadhouse, he'd seen exactly zero cars. The only sound apart from his trainers slapping the bitumen was the occasional squawk from the ever-present crows. Could it be possible that he'd somehow ended up on a private road? He hefted his guitar and looked over his shoulder. Closely-packed trees crowded the road in both directions. Tottie had driven in this direction, so it had to lead somewhere.

His mind began to throw up what ifs. *What if no one comes along and it starts to get dark? What if I walk for hours and the road disappears into the bush? What if I'm walking in a circle and whichever way I turn takes me back to the roadhouse?* He forced himself to stop and get a grip. He pulled his phone out and checked the screen. Nothing. Tottie really did a job on it.

Without the phone, he couldn't even tell the time. Staring up at the cloudless autumn sky, he guessed it was early afternoon. He'd had a couple of slices of pizza the night before, making it nearly fourteen hours since he'd last eaten. If someone didn't come along soon, he thought he might lie down by the side of the road and let the birds eat him.

A crow screeched down from a nearby peppermint tree as if to beckon him over. Tommy laughed, but the sound echoed back off the deserted road like a ghostly moan.

"Okay." He spoke to the crow. "I'm starting to spook myself." He stopped walking and waited for the bird to respond. The shiny black creature remained silent, turning its head to the side as if listening to something only winged creatures could hear.

A second later, Tommy heard the rumbling of an ancient engine. He dropped his guitar and spun around. Sure enough, the old green Holden Ute he'd spotted at the roadhouse came barrelling towards him. The afternoon sun glinted off the bull bar, sending out flashes of gold and silver bright enough to make him shade his eyes.

"Yes." Tommy let out a whoop of pleasure and stuck out his thumb. "Come on, lady, do the right thing." He took a couple of steps backwards, holding his breath.

The Holden drew closer, almost alongside him with no sign of slowing. Tommy's heart thumped harder. He forced his face into a look that he hoped was more hapless musician than serial killer. He had the urge to scream for the car to stop but swallowed it and kept his thumb up.

The Ute blew past him, kicking up a flurry of twigs and loose gravel. He watched the back of the vehicle with a feeling of resignation. Nothing had gone right since the moment he slunk out on Adeline like a thief in the night. What did he expect?

When the orange brake lights snapped on and the Ute came to a stop, Tommy thought he was hallucinating. But there it was, clear as glass and twice as lovely. The classic Holden was waiting for him like a beautiful mirage.

Tommy snatched up his guitar and raced towards the vehicle, half expecting it to waver and disappear. *God, I must have smoked some heavy shit.* He laughed out loud and picked up his feet.

When he reached the passenger's window, the grin died on his lips. A large woman with short dark hair stared out at him. He experienced the same moment of unease as that when he'd once stood in an empty auditorium. That absence of noise and activity was reflected in the woman's eyes. Her bottom lip jutted forward, giving her a bullish appearance. The words of gratitude he'd rehearsed on the short run evaporated, leaving him stumbling for something to say.

"Need a lift?" Another woman, the one he remembered seeing at the roadhouse, leaned forward from the driver's seat.

"I…" He stole another glance at the silent woman in the passenger's seat. For one crazy moment, he almost turned her down, but desperation got the better of him. "Yes, I'm trying to get to Busselton." It was the first town that popped into his head.

The driver took her time answering, looking him over like he was a prize pig. *Can't blame her, two women on their own picking up a hitchhiker, they're bound to be cautious.* It fleetingly occurred to him that picking up a hitchhiker was an odd thing for them to do in the first place, but the idea of being stranded at nightfall chased his doubts away.

"I can take you as far as the highway, but then you're on your own." There was a curtness to the offer that suggested he make his mind up or be left behind.

"Great. Thanks." He looked at the bed of the Ute, unsure where she meant for him to sit.

"Toss your gear in the back, then you can ride up front. There's plenty of room."

* * *

The cab wasn't as roomy as the woman seemed to think. After some shuffling around, Tommy found himself flanked by the two women with the gear stick between his legs like an extra penis.

"I'm Lizzy, Lizzy Hatcher, and that's Soona." She jerked her thumb towards the woman on Tommy's left.

143

"I'm Tommy Brass. Thanks for stopping." The air in the cab was stale, as if they never put the windows down. He could smell something mouldy, a thick scent that filled his mouth. Still, it was better than being stranded.

The engine missed a few revs then spluttered to life. Lizzy gripped the gearstick, her arm almost touching Tommy's leg.

"Friends in Busselton?" Lizzy asked without taking her eyes off the road.

Tommy wondered if it were a good idea to tell them he was destitute and that there was nothing waiting for him in Busselton but a night sleeping in a doorway. How would the women react? They might offer him money or peg him for a bum and kick him out of the Ute.

"No." He drew out the word. "I'm actually trying to make my way home to Melbourne, but I'm a bit short on funds."

He watched Lizzy's reaction. If she was surprised by his response, she didn't show it. He looked down at his stained T-shirt, realising it didn't take a genius to work out he was in dire straits.

"I can give you a few days' work." Her voice was deep for a woman's, almost gruff. "The roof on one of my sheds needs mending."

Tommy's mind ticked through the possibilities. If he took her up on the offer, it would cost him two days. On the other hand, he might be able to get enough money together for the bus fare to Melbourne. The bus would take time, three days at least. Five days in total. That still left him with time to do a little busking in Busselton, maybe scrape together enough for a cheap flight.

She was waiting for a response. He wondered if she'd be offended if he asked what she was willing to pay. "Um." He rubbed his hand across the back of his neck. "How much. I mean, what sort of pay?"

She pulled her eyes away from the road and raised her eyebrows. "I can pay two hundred and fifty dollars plus two night's room and board." She glanced down at his dirty shirt.

He opened his mouth to answer when the vehicle hit a pothole. Without a seatbelt, Tommy bounced so high, his head touched the roof of the cab. He grabbed on to the edge of the seat for balance, his hand brushing Lizzy's companion's leg. She jerked away from his touch as if stung.

"Sorry." He turned to look at the silent woman. Her eyes were fixed on the window.

"Well?" Lizzy sounded impatient.

He supposed he could put up with the odd pair for a couple of days. "Yes. Thanks. Sounds good."

Chapter Three

The Holden veered right, turning off onto a narrow side road. Tommy tried to read the street sign, but the post was askew, and by the time he located the actual sign, the name was out of view. Not that it mattered where he was. As long as Lizzy dropped him off on the highway, he'd find his way to Busselton or Bunbury. Anywhere he could catch a bus to the city.

The narrow road was an uneven line with dense bush on either side. Sunlight cut through the tops of the trees, spilling jagged lines of light on the worn bitumen. Tommy scrunched forward, his crotch almost touching the gearstick, and pulled his phone out of his back pocket. It was dry, but sticky from being dunked in cola. He tried touching the screen, but the thing was dead.

"That won't do you any good out here," Lizzy spoke for the first time in ten minutes. "Mobile phones don't work in this area."

Tommy wondered if it was his imagination or whether there was something threatening in the way she spoke.

He'd been quick to accept her offer of work, not even wondering about who else might live at the house.

"So." Tommy shoved the phone back in his pocket. "Will I be helping your husband with the shed?"

Lizzy gave a grunt. "If you're trying to ask if there's anyone else at the house, the answer is no. It's just me and Soona." She glanced in his direction. "And now you."

"Okay. Great." He tried to hide his relief. They were just two aging women looking for a bit of help around the house. He felt himself relax a little, deciding a few days working in the country air might be just what he needed before heading home.

Five minutes later, the house came into view. Tommy let out a whistle. It certainly wasn't what he'd been expecting. The place was a monster: a three-storey mansion, like something out of an old movie. Fancy metal work around the eaves and an old-style wrap around veranda.

"Nice."

"Glad you approve." Lizzy's response was curt. "This," she said, nodding towards the building, "is Mable House."

She pulled the Ute around to the side of the building and turned off the engine. Tommy waited while Soona climbed out of the cab, then followed. Standing next to her, he was struck by the size of the woman. She had to be almost one hundred and eighty centimetres – around six feet tall.

"This way." Lizzy was already on the move, talking over her shoulder.

Tommy grabbed his gear from the back and dashed after her. Up close, he could see the place was pretty run-

147

down and in need of major work. Flaking paint on the iron latticework, sagging veranda, and crumbling bricks gave the place an almost derelict look. If the house was this bad, he shuddered to think what condition the shed was in. Suddenly, two hundred and fifty dollars didn't seem like such a great offer.

He watched Lizzy stride through the long grass and round the corner, deciding if the job was too much, he'd just sneak away in the early morning. At least that way he'd get a meal and a night's sleep.

"That's the shed." Lizzy pointed across the backyard.

Tommy noticed a couple of dilapidated structures just beyond a Hills Hoist rotary clothes line. On the right stood a wire mesh chook pen. The smell of chicken poo was strong and mixed with something else, a sharp odour he couldn't quite identify.

"Which one do you want me to work on?" Tommy eyed the sheds with a sinking feeling growing in his gut. The idea of sneaking away while the two women were asleep seemed more and more appealing.

"The back one." As if sensing his concern, she added, "Don't worry. All you need to do is patch up the roof."

"Okay. Great." He heard himself using the same response over and over, as if *okay* and *great* were all he could say. *She must think I'm a real idiot.*

He heard movement behind him and turned. Soona stood a few metres away, silent and staring. Tommy guessed the woman had something wrong with her, autism or something like that. Her vacant stare made him uncomfortable, eager to be away from the woman. When Lizzy turned and climbed the rickety stairs to the back door, he followed, glad to be on the move.

Inside, they walked through a covered veranda packed with old cartons and boxes. Tommy thought he could smell mouse pee, but it could have just been mildew. Lizzy led him into the old-fashioned kitchen dominated by a huge oak table. Everywhere he looked was cluttered with old clocks and faded photos of stern-looking men and women.

Tommy noticed some sort of needlework picture above the stove with the words *THE HEART OF HEAVEN IS THE HOME*. He almost laughed. Mable House was big, but not what he'd call heavenly. He caught Lizzy watching him and realised he was smiling.

"Something funny?" She had her hands on her hips. She was a large woman, not as big as Soona, but strong-looking. Her mouth was puckered into a tight, angry circle.

"No. No. I just like the picture. Did you do it?" He hoped the words held the right amount of sincerity.

She held his gaze for a second and then turned. "This way." She walked through the kitchen, ignoring his question.

Lizzy led him through a large sitting room where all the furniture was covered in dusty sheets. From there, they crossed a tiled foyer with a wide staircase. On the right of the stairs sat an antique lift.

"Wow." Tommy couldn't help being impressed. He'd only ever seen old places like it on TV. "Was this place once a hotel?"

Lizzy stopped walking and turned around. He could tell by the look on her face he'd offended her again. "This *place*." She spoke slowly. "Mable House has been many things over the years. Mostly a hospital."

Tommy almost said "Okay, great," but stopped himself just in time. Instead he nodded and kept his mouth shut. At least that way he couldn't upset or insult the woman.

Lizzy led him to a small room on the left of the stairs. "This is where you'll stay." She pointed at a narrow single bed as if training a dog. "I want you outside in ten minutes so I can show you where to start in the morning." The loud, commanding tone of her voice was really starting to wear on his nerves.

If the falling-down shed hadn't convinced him that coming to Mable House was a bad idea, then Lizzy's attitude certainly did the trick. He nodded and smiled even though he had no intention of still being around in the morning.

Once the door closed behind Lizzy, Tommy let out a long, deep breath. He sat on the squeaky bed and looked around the depressing little room. He had twenty-five dollars in his wallet and a broken phone, was he really going to skip out on the chance to earn some money just because the old woman was rude to him? His mind went back to the fight with Tottie at the roadhouse. He saw her lower the window and throw the cup of cola over him. He felt a mixture of anger and shame so sharp, it was as if he were back in that humiliating moment. Would a few days with two crazy women be worse than putting up with Tottie?

"Damn." He pounded the pillow with his fist. He decided to give it one day. If by tomorrow night things were intolerable, he'd sneak away and head for the highway.

Chapter Four

They ate dinner in silence. Careful to only snatch sideways glances, Tommy watched the two women demolish their food. Not that he was any more civilised. When Lizzy slapped down his plate of mash potatoes and beef stew, it was all he could do to not start shovelling the food into his mouth using his hands.

The food turned out to be bland, the beef chewy, but Tommy didn't care. He ate every scrap along with a few slices of homemade bread which he used to sop up the dregs. By the time he put his knife and fork down, his sides were aching.

He was the first one to speak. "That was a great meal. Thanks."

Lizzy nodded, but Soona continued to chew with her mouth half open – thick, hairy arms moving up and down as she devoured at least six slices of bread. Apart from the clank of cutlery on china, the only other sound was the ticking of multiple clocks.

What Tommy really wanted was to get back to his room and play a little music on his guitar. It had been months since he'd written anything. The last time he'd actually penned a song was a few days before Adeline told him about the baby. Thinking about Adeline put him in mind of his phone, and suddenly he needed to see her picture.

"Um… Lizzy, do you have any rice?"

She stopped eating and frowned. Tommy noticed her eyes were a strange colour, pale like a rain puddle on a bleak winter's day. Pinned under her cold gaze, he almost lost his train of thought.

"Are you trying to tell me you're still hungry?" There were small specks of food lodged in the corners of her mouth.

Tommy covered a laugh with a forced cough, hoping she didn't notice his amusement. "No. My phone's wet, I want to put it in some rice to dry it out." He pulled his phone out and set it on the table.

She let out a tired breath and pointed her fork at the sleek black mobile. "I told you, that thing won't do you any good here. You can use the phone." She jerked a thumb over her shoulder to an old-fashioned rotary-style phone sitting on a fancy table with velvet cushions. "Nothing long-distance, we don't have money to waste on telephone bills."

"Yes, thanks. But if I can dry it out, there are other functions I can use. Photos, clock, torch." He gave her what he hoped was a winning smile. When that didn't work, he tried playing on her sympathy. "I just like to look at pictures of my family."

Lizzy dropped her fork, letting it hit the plate with a sharp *clang*. She turned to Soona and plucked a half-eaten slice of bread out of the woman's hand. "You've had enough."

Tommy watched Soona's eyes drift away from her plate and fix on something in the corner of the room. He forced his face to remain neutral. If he didn't need the money, he would have loved to tell Lizzy to back off. One thing he couldn't stand was a bully.

Lizzy stood. "Clear the table." For a second, Tommy thought she was speaking to him. Before he could react, Soona got up and began shuffling around gathering the plates, a glassy-eyed look fixed on her face.

Lizzy banged open a few cupboards before dumping a bowl and a large bag of rice in front of him. "Here."

In the time it took Tommy to open the rice, fill the bowl, and submerge his phone, Lizzy prepared three cups of hot tea. He thought about telling her he didn't drink tea, but decided not to risk causing another angry outburst. Instead, he picked up the murky-looking drink and swallowed it down in two gulps, wincing at the sugary aftertaste.

* * *

The sound of a bird's cry, shrill and urgent, startled Tommy from sleep. He screwed up his eyes expecting a blast of snoring from Tottie. In the few seconds between sleep and wakefulness, he couldn't quite remember where he was. It was only the sight of shabby blue curtains, half closed over a grimy little window, that reminded him of the previous night.

Mable House, how could he forget the two kooky women and the crumbling hospital? *Mental hospital, most likely*. He sat up and the room took a sickening lurch to the left. His head felt fuzzy, as if filled with mud; it reminded him of his nights spent partying in Margaret River. The sour taste coating his tongue suggested a hangover. He ran his fingers through his hair as if trying to massage his brain into action and realised his hands were trembling.

He hadn't had a drink in almost two days, it had to be food poisoning or a mild flu. Going over the events of the previous evening, he tried to remember if he'd felt unwell. Beyond eating dinner, he couldn't recall anything – not even going to bed. Another more disturbing thought occurred to him. Could he be experiencing alcohol withdrawal? He remembered watching a movie about an alcoholic. The guy stopped drinking and by the next day he was vomiting and shaking. Tommy swallowed back a rush of saliva. Had he sunk that low? Was he an alcoholic?

Scrambling off the bed, he headed for the small bathroom on legs that felt like wet spaghetti. The face that stared back at him in the small rust-speckled mirror looked washed out and gaunt. "Jesus." His voice was thick, almost unrecognisable.

He filled up the small basin and used a cracked bar of yellow soap he found on the floor to wash his face. Then, plunging his head into the sink, he rubbed soap through his greasy blond hair. He turned on the cold water and rinsed his head, gasping with shock as the freezing liquid hit his skin. When he was done, he pulled off his dirty T-shirt and used it to dry himself.

He checked his reflection, teeth chattering. Still sickly, but at least he was clean. There was nothing he could do about the two days of stubble on his chin, but hopefully he smelled a bit fresher. Maybe it was a good thing that he was broke. Better to detox now and be clean when he met with the record company guy. And Adeline.

As he picked through his pack looking for something to wear, he let his mind dwell on his wife. After everything they'd been through together, years of living week to week as he pursued his dreams of becoming a recording star, she'd stuck by him. Then when she needed him... He felt another wave of nausea, this time brought on by the guilt and shame of realising what a coward he'd turned into. When she told him about the baby, he knew he had to leave. Letting her go was the only thing he could do for her. The only way to give the baby a chance at a better life, one that didn't involve grimy bars and weeks on the road. No, they deserved better than he could give.

He put on a red T-shirt and raked his fingers through his hair. Everything would change when he got home. He'd find a way to make things right with Adeline, no matter what it took.

* * *

After a shaky start, Tommy made it up the ladder. He still felt bleary-eyed and slightly nauseated, but the fresh air seemed to be helping. He picked up a half-a-metre piece of timber and began hammering it in place. The roof was in pretty bad shape, but he was making good progress. Like most struggling musicians, he'd worked his fair share of odd jobs – including construction.

As he worked, his mind kept drifting back to Adeline. The decision to go home and beg her to take him back took root. Even the idea of being a father felt less terrifying. Who knew, maybe he'd even be good at it. Tommy felt his stomach flip, not from nausea this time, but excitement. He'd make sure he wowed the record execs. This was his chance to give his wife and baby the life they deserved. Without realising it, he began singing.

He'd finished almost half the left side of the roof by the time he noticed the heat. His shirt was soaked with sweat, clinging to his skin like a layer of plaster. Hours of bending left him with a dull ache in his side and the small of his back. Peeling his shirt off, he glanced down into the yard. Below, near the foot of the ladder, he spotted Soona. The woman was dressed like the world's biggest toddler in denim overalls over a yellow sweatshirt.

The sight of her cross-legged on the grass knocked a memory loose: Lizzy snatching food out of the woman's hand. Had that really happened or was it a weird dream brought on by his alcohol withdrawal?

He tucked his shirt in the back of his jeans, hitched his leg over the ladder, and climbed down. "Hi, Soona." He noticed her rocking back and forth and wondered if she could even hear him.

Shrugging, Tommy headed for the house in search of a cold drink. Lizzy was nowhere to be found, so he helped himself to a glass of tap water which he drank in one go, standing over the sink. He was about to refill the glass when he noticed a bowl of rice on the cracked Formica counter. Another fragment of the previous evening fell into place. He remembered asking for the rice so he could dry his phone.

He plunged his fingers into the rice but couldn't feel the phone. Rubbing the back of his neck, he tried to fill in the missing pieces of his memory. Maybe the phone was somewhere in his room. He considered going to look for it but decided it could wait. The sooner he finished the roof, the quicker he'd be on his way home.

As soon as he opened the back door, Tommy heard the humming. Soona still sitting close to the ladder with her hands near her ears, fingers wiggling. There was no mistaking the tune – *You Are My Sunshine*. He'd been singing the song all morning.

Tommy sat on the overgrown lawn, wincing as a cramp travelled up his back. He took a breath and the pain evaporated. He began humming in time with the woman. Soona continued to hum and wiggle her fingers, showing no awareness of his presence. After a minute or so, he began singing. It was a corny song, but Adeline loved it, so that made it Tommy's favourite. To his surprise, Soona joined in. She could only manage the words *sunshine* and *happy*, humming through the rest of the lyrics.

It felt good to reach someone with his voice, even if it was an audience of one. In spite of waking up feeling like hell, his voice was in good form, and singing for the pure joy of it lifted his spirits, making all the crap he'd been through over the last week seem unimportant. If everything panned out, he might get the chance to sing to his son or daughter just like he was doing now with Soona.

Tommy opened his mouth to sing the last verse when an explosion cut through the air. The sound, louder than thunder, rang in his ears like someone had clanged a cymbal next to his head. He clamped his hands over his ears and looked around. Lizzy stood at the foot of the back stairs, a shotgun clamped to her shoulder.

Soona scrambled to her feet, hands flapping wildly. Over the ringing in his head, Tommy could hear the woman bleating like an injured sheep. Lizzy let the gun drop down. Clamping it in the crook of her arm, she walked towards him. For one crazy moment, he thought she meant to shoot him. He stumbled back, hands in the air. Lizzy gave him a disgusted look and walked towards the chook pen.

"What the hell are you doing?" Once the immediate threat of being shot evaporated, Tommy felt a rush of anger. "You could have taken our heads off."

Lizzy reached the pen and bent over. She stood, holding what looked like a fox by the tail. The dead animal dangled from her hand, its tongue lolling out the side of its mouth.

"Can't let a fox run loose in the hen house." She held the creature up near her face. "Something like this can do a lot of damage."

Still reeling from what just happened, Tommy watched open-mouthed as Lizzy walked towards him. Behind her, chooks squawked and fluttered in a panicky frenzy.

She stopped a metre or so away from him and tossed the fox to the ground at his feet. It landed with a dull *thump*. "I'm not paying you to take your clothes off and sing."

Soona continued to bleat and flap. Lizzy's hand shot out with lightning speed, slapping the terrified woman on the cheek. "Go check the cows have water." Her voice was deep, vibrating with anger.

"Hey." Tommy grabbed Lizzy's arm. "What's the matter with you? Don't do that."

Almost as quickly as she'd lashed out at Soona, Lizzy had the shotgun up and pointed at him. Instinctively, Tommy stepped back and held up his hands.

"I'm sorry." Tommy watched Lizzy's pale eyes narrow over the top of the gun. "Please, don't shoot."

For a second there was silence save the sound of fluttering wings from the chook pen. When Lizzy finally lowered the gun, Tommy let out a relieved breath. His heart was hammering so fast, he thought his legs might give out under the strain.

"I wasn't going to." She spat out the words, white foam gathering in the corners of her mouth. "You shouldn't have interfered. When you grabbed me, I thought..." She trailed off, her eyes darting between the ground and the chook pen. In that moment, he could see a resemblance between her and Soona and wondered if they were sisters.

"I'm sorry." He'd backed up until his heels touched the ladder. He didn't dare do anything to provoke her, not while she still had the shotgun hanging from the crook of her arm. "Really. I shouldn't have grabbed you."

She made a clicking sound with her tongue, pale eyes searching his face. He had the impression she was sizing him up. It occurred to him that no one knew where he was. A chill worked its way up his spine, turning the sweat on his back to icy trickles.

"I'm a nurse. I help people, I don't shoot them." As suddenly as the whole drama began, it was over. Lizzy stormed off towards the house. Soona was nowhere to be seen.

Tommy swiped at his forehead. His arm came away wet with sweat. If not for the dead fox lying on the ground, it would have been easy to believe he'd imagined the crazy scene. He knew Lizzy was strange, but nothing had prepared him for the sudden violent outburst. For a few minutes he'd actually feared for his life.

He should leave. Grab his stuff and start walking. He sat on the ladder, mostly because his legs were still shaky. What, he wondered, would Lizzy do if she saw him trying to leave? She was a strong-looking woman, but she had to be in her fifties. If something started, he could easily overpower her. But did he want to risk a confrontation? She was a crack shot with the gun, he'd seen her hit the fox from ten metres away.

Once again, he decided to take the coward's way out: wait until night and sneak away. He'd lose out on the money she'd promised him, but that couldn't be helped. He'd just have to come up with a new plan. On the bright side, the long walk to the highway would give him plenty of time to think.

* * *

Making it through dinner was harder the second time. Tommy had no appetite for the boiled carrots and meatloaf Lizzy served with a generous smothering of watery gravy. Pushing the food around his plate made his stomach clench into a tight ball as the stench of burnt fat hung in the air like a gassy cloud.

When the plates were cleared away, Lizzy made three cups of sugary tea. Tommy forced himself to take a few sips. "Have you seen my phone?" He set the cup down; it clanked against his plate.

The question hung in the air. Lizzy continued to sip from her cup as if he hadn't spoken. It seemed she was intent on ignoring him, but after another slow mouthful, she finally put her cup down and spoke.

"You said you were going to put it in rice." She jerked her chin towards the counter where the bowl of dry rice still sat.

Tommy followed her gaze. "Yes, I checked, but it's not there." He tried to keep his tone light, remembering the way her washed-out eyes regarded him over the barrel of the shotgun.

She wiped her mouth with the back of her hand and shrugged. The gesture seemed overly casual for a woman as intense as Lizzy. He had the distinct feeling she was lying. But why would she take his phone? Without making an accusation, there was little more he could do.

"Right." He started to stand. The cramp in his lower back gripped him like a clamp, only this time the pain spiralled around his stomach.

"Are you okay?" Lizzy's face wavered. Her mouth looked huge.

Tommy opened his lips. "My... My stomach." He grasped the edge of the table but couldn't quite hold on.

When he hit the floor, something crunched under his arm. He was aware of a high-pitched sheep-like bleating sound and then his vision darkened.

"Tommy." Someone called his name. He opened his eyes. The pain took his breath away. He grunted through gritted teeth. "Keep your eyes open," Lizzy barked at him. "Does it help when I press here?"

He felt pressure on his stomach and the pain diminished. He nodded. She took her hand away and a shaft of agony cut through his gut. He screamed and grabbed at her hand. Faces floated above him, coming in and out of focus.

"Have you felt sick or had any pain today?" Lizzy was asking him something, but the words were running together in his brain. The top of his head burned as if his hair was on fire.

"What's happening to me?" He managed to get the words out around panicked breaths.

Lizzy clamped her hand on his forehead. The iciness of her touch made him jump. "I think it's appendicitis. We need to get you to the hospital." He watched her cross the room and reach for the phone.

He turned his head to the left. Soona stood near the sink, her mouth opening and closing as if she were whispering. Thoughts jumped around in his brain. *Am I dying? Why now? I can't die without telling Adeline why I left.*

"Damn." Lizzy reappeared beside him. "The phone's not working." She shook her head. "I'm not surprised. I've had the men from Comm Tec out twice this year but it's always something." Her eyes narrowed. "You'd think two women on their own out here would be a priority, but do those bigwigs care about country people?" She continued to talk as if they were sitting next to each other on a bus stop bench.

"Please." Tommy grabbed her hand. "Do something, the pain."

Lizzy frowned and pulled her hand free. "There's nothing I can do. You won't make it to the hospital in the Ute." She jabbed a finger into his stomach, making him howl like a baby. "See. Jostling you over country roads in my old bus will only make it worse. When that thing ruptures, it'll kill you. And looking at your symptoms, I'd say it's about to happen."

Tommy couldn't believe what he was hearing. The room wavered as his eyes filled with tears. His teeth were chattering so hard, his gums ached. He opened his mouth to beg for help when something buzzed in his brain and the lights went out.

Chapter Five

A tap dripped, wet plops echoed on what sounded like tiles. Tommy squinted. A stark light shone directly into his eyes. The pain in his gut was a hot pulse of agony. The sharp, acid scent of bleach stung his nostrils. *I'm in a hospital.* In spite of the pain, he let out a relieved breath.

"You had a seizure." Lizzy's face appeared above him, temporarily blocking the light.

His mind tried to fathom what was happening. Why was Lizzy still with him? Surely the doctors would tell her to wait outside.

"Are we at the hospital?" His lips felt thick, sloppy.

Lizzy frowned. "I told you, Mable House *is* a hospital." She leaned closer. Her breath smelled like cheese that had been left in the sun. "Now, I'm not making any promises, but I'm going to try and get your appendix out before it kills you."

The word hit him like a punch. Did she really mean to cut him open? He tried to sit up, but something pinned him to the spot. Tommy craned his neck, looking down the length of his body. A strap ran across his chest, another restrained his thighs. His T-shirt was gone, his jeans and underwear pulled down around his knees. Completely exposed, he shivered.

"Soona." Lizzy turned away and spoke. "Bring the trolley closer."

A metallic rattle followed by a *clang*. Tommy strained against the straps, the tendons in his neck tightening. "No. No, you can't operate on me." The numbness of his lips made speaking difficult. His body moved sluggishly but his heart hammered like a race horse.

Lizzy loomed over him. "You asked for my help, so I'm giving it." There was a flat quality to her voice, as if the decision had been made.

"I don't want your help." Tommy tried to twist away from her, but the movement was weak, without effect. Something cold touched his stomach. "Oh God." He pushed out a scream.

"Stop it." She snapped off the words, her tone similar to the way she spoke to Soona when ordering her around. "I'm going to give you a local; it should take care of most of the pain."

Most? He closed his eyes and saw himself running down the road, dumping his guitar in the back of the old Holden Ute. He heard Lizzy's voice talking about his mobile phone. *That won't do you any good out here.* Something was wrong in Mable House. What she was proposing to do was the stuff of madness.

He stopped struggling and opened his eyes. "I don't want you to operate on me." He tried to make his voice sound calm, reasonable. "I'll take my chances in the back of the Ute."

She was bending over him. A sharp sting in his belly. The woman wasn't listening. *She's not wearing gloves.* It was a stupid thought, why would she be wearing gloves? *It's not like she's a doctor.*

"You're not a doctor." This time his lips worked. The words echoed off the ceiling. Tommy let out a shriek that sounded very similar to the way Soona bleated when Lizzy shot the fox.

A pulling sensation in his abdomen and then buzzing in his brain, hot and angry. Bile filled his mouth and nose. Just as the world melted into red, Tommy heard Lizzy speak.

"Uh-oh. That's not good." The buzzing intensified and then blackness took him.

* * *

Adeline was making coffee. He could smell the rich, dark liquid even in the bedroom. Tommy couldn't be bothered opening his eyes. He'd wait until she brought the cup through and put it next to the bed. When she leaned over to kiss him, he'd pull her back into bed and they'd spend the morning fooling around. Her long, dark hair touched his chest, tickling just below his heart. For some reason, he wanted to cry.

The tickle turned into a scratch as if rough fingers were tugging at him. Tommy opened his eyes. "Addie?" His mouth moved, but the words were stuck in a painful lump at the back of his throat.

A face hovered above him, blurry and out of focus. He blinked dry, sore eyes and the shape coalesced into clarity. "You're awake." Lizzy made a clicking sound with her tongue and fiddled with his shirt.

Tommy tried to look down and see what she was doing, but his neck refused to cooperate. Lifting his hand, he grabbed her wrist. She pulled away as if stung and his fingers hit the bed. He was in a different room. The ceiling was cracked and yellowing with age. Fighting the pain in his throat, he turned his head to the right.

Sunlight, yellow and warm-looking, shone through a small window draped in yellow, ruffled curtains. He caught sight of a snatch of blue. He was seeing the sky. *I'm alive. Whatever she did to me, I lived through it and I'm seeing the sky.* His heart threw a weird, dipping sensation.

"I'm giving you something to help with the pain. It'll make you a bit groggy."

He turned back and watched Lizzy slide a long, thin needle into his bicep. There was a tube attached to his arm, and clear liquid travelled from a bag suspended on a tall metal stand. If not for the shabby room, the equipment looked like it belonged in a real hospital. Lizzy was a bit loopy, but she seemed to know what she was doing. *I'm alive.* The words kept popping back into his mind as if he couldn't quite believe it was true.

A warm sensation washed over him, a pleasant feeling like leaning back into a soothing bath. He closed his eyes and allowed the warmth to engulf him. Outside the window, a bird sang, a happy sound that reminded him of a Disney movie.

* * *

"You're awake then?" Lizzy's voice woke him with a start.

Tommy pressed his palms down and pulled himself up on the bed. As he did so, Lizzy leaned over him and propped a pillow behind his back. He noticed she was dressed in a navy shirt and dark pants, a departure from her usual dark jeans and floral blouse. The outfit made her look more nurse-like. He wondered if that was the look she was going for. Or maybe it was her uniform. She never did tell him what sort of hospital he was in.

He opened his mouth to ask, but she held up a hand to silence him. "Don't try to speak. Your throat will be a bit sore, better to rest it for now." At the mention of his throat, a quiver of panic blossomed in his chest.

He couldn't afford to have his voice compromised, not with the record company meeting coming up. Thinking about the meeting, he tried to remember how many days he had left before he had to be in Melbourne. He thought of asking Lizzy about the date, but remembered what she said about his voice.

She picked something up off the metal locker next to the bed. Tommy watched her fitting a new bag of liquid onto the stand. The drugs she'd given him earlier were starting to wear off. The pain in his gut wasn't too bad, but it *was* throbbing. He swallowed and grimaced. A hard, jagged knot sat in the back of his throat. The quiver of panic turned into a galloping horse, rushing through his mind at breakneck speed.

He put his fingers to his throat and felt a thick layer of bandaging. In spite of Lizzy's warning, he tried to speak. "Wh…" The word lodged behind the obstruction in his throat, and a metallic taste coated his tongue.

"I told you, don't talk." Lizzy dashed around the bed and flung open a narrow door. Her head disappeared into a cupboard. She returned to his side and stuck a metal kidney-shaped bowl in his hand. "Spit in this."

Tommy held the bowl to his mouth and a glob of viscous-looking blood dropped from his lips, hitting the pan with a meaty *plop*. He stared at the gooey mess, unable to drag his eyes away from the pea-sized lump.

"You had a seizure… Several seizures." He heard her speaking, but the glob of blood had him hypnotised. "I'd already made the incision, it was just as I thought, your appendix *had* ruptured." She let out a breath. "Anyway, you vomited and started choking. I did my best but I couldn't clear your airway, so I had to perform an emergency tracheotomy."

Tommy looked up and caught Lizzy off guard. There was something guilty in the way her pale grey eyes flicked around the room. She'd seen him catch her unease, he could tell by the way she flicked out her tongue and licked her lips.

"I did what I could." Her tone was truculent now, daring him to question her skills. "You're lucky to be alive." He had the feeling there was something more she wasn't telling him. *As if butchering my throat wasn't enough.*

He wanted to ask questions. *What about my voice? Will I be able to sing?* And most of all he wanted to know what he was, if not a singer? Not that Lizzy could answer that one.

"Soona's working on the Ute. As soon as she gets it going, I'll drive you to Bunbury Hospital."

He let his head fall back against the metal bed frame. Whatever strength he had left ebbed away. Tears trickled from the corner of his eyes, cold against his feverish skin. Singing was all he was good at. The one thing he could do – it was who he was. Without his voice, she may as well have cut into his heart.

Lizzy bent over the bed and settled the sheets around his waist. He watched the back of her head through blurry eyes. The skin on her crown was pink against the thick, coarse grey hair that grew in limp swirls. The urge to curl his fist into a ball and smash it down on her skull gripped him with surprising speed and urgency. She'd taken everything from him, maybe he should give her a taste of her own medicine. Wasn't medicine what all this was about? Lizzy's brand of medicine – kill or cure. *No*, he corrected himself. Kill, cure, or butcher.

"All right." She straightened and adjusted the hem of her shirt. "I'll be back in about an hour with something for the pain. You hang onto the bowl in case you need it."

He stared into her eyes, feeling a tiny spark of satisfaction when she looked away. There was more than guilt behind her washed-out eyes, but what that was he had no idea. For the most part, he no longer cared.

Without a watch, it was difficult to tell, but Tommy guessed it was an hour or more before Lizzy reappeared. This time, she didn't have much to say. What was the point? He couldn't answer her. She gave him another injection in his bicep. When the point of the needle pierced his skin, he let out a sigh of relief. The wave of euphoria that accompanied the injection was all he had to look forward to. That and the sleep that followed. Tommy wished the injection was poison, anything to end the misery.

* * *

The pain in his gut jerked him from sleep. Hair plastered to his forehead with sweat, Tommy sat forward. The last thing he remembered was wishing she'd poison him. Judging by the pain cramping his stomach and the nausea, she'd done just that.

He pulled himself into a sitting position, but quickly realised the new angle only made the pain worse. Half lying, propped on one elbow, he grabbed the kidney dish from the locker. The metal tray in his hand, Tommy opened his mouth. Retching and moaning as vomit hit his injured throat, he leaned over the bowl, letting sour yellow bile spill out. He tried to put the dish back on the locker, but his hand trembled so badly, it slipped from his fingers, hitting the floor with a *clang*.

Spots of light, red and orange, danced in front of his eyes. *What's happening to me?* He slumped back on the pillow, breathless and dizzy. He tried to remember what Lizzy said about the crude surgery, but his mind burned with images of thick bush and rusty knives. Words danced around in his head, *ruptured, seizure – I made the incision*. She'd tried to tell him something went wrong. He'd been so caught up in the possibility of losing his voice, he hadn't taken anything else in. *Am I dying?*

Heart hammering like a drum, Tommy clamped his hands over his eyes. If something went wrong, why wasn't he in a hospital? As much as he wanted to blame her for his predicament, he knew the woman was trying to care for him. Lizzy was strange, but he thought she genuinely wanted to help, so wouldn't the logical thing be to rush him to a hospital? Did Lizzy think along logical lines?

He pulled his hands away from his eyes and looked towards the window. The light bled from gold to orange. The sun was setting. He was no doctor, but he could feel his body struggling. Every movement was pain, but he couldn't just lie in bed and wait for death. He'd been so ready to give up a few hours ago. The thought of never singing again seemed like a death sentence, but now the real possibility of death loomed over him like a giant black bird, wings outstretched, throwing his earlier fears into nothing more than a thin shadow.

He wanted to live. He wanted to live with Adeline and his baby, nothing else mattered. Tommy threw back the covers and grabbed hold of the tube taped to the crook of his arm. He tugged the bung. A sliding sensation then a jab of fire. The needle came away with a trickle of blood.

Standing threw him off balance. His bare feet slipped as if he were on the bow of a ship in rough weather. Taking care to avoid the puddle of vomit beside the bed, Tommy lurched towards the door. The three steps it took to reach the door and yank it open were awkward and rolling, but he persevered.

Once he had the door open, Tommy stopped and leaned on the frame. Sweat ran down the back of his neck, soaking the old-man pyjamas Lizzy had dressed him in. He was leaving. If he had to crawl all the way back to the roadhouse, he'd do it. *God, don't let it come to that.* If he could get downstairs, he'd swipe the car keys and see if the Ute really was playing up. With any luck, he'd get the old bomb started and be on his way to a real hospital in an hour.

Using the wall to steady himself, Tommy started down the hall. It took a few seconds for the reality of his situation to sink in. He was upstairs. Why didn't he realise that before? The blue sky, the sound of Lizzy's heavy footfalls on the stairs – why hadn't he realised? *Because I'm out of my head with pain.*

"Shit." He propped himself up against the wall. *Now what?*

The way he saw it, there were two options: the stairs or the lift. Not knowing if the ancient contraption worked *or* how to use it narrowed his choices. He'd have to go for the stairs.

Tommy willed his legs to keep moving. Bare feet sliding over the dusty boards in a slow, sifting rhythm, he reached the staircase. The first few steps were a balancing act, his vision going in and out of focus while rubbery legs threatened to fold. Only by clinging to the rail and concentrating more on feel than sight did he make it to the halfway mark.

He allowed himself a break, gripping the handrail with both hands for fear of tipping forward. The throbbing in his gut intensified, keeping time with his heart. Nausea washed another spill of bile up over his throat, this time so sudden that he could do nothing but let it spew out onto his chin and chest. He was crying now, with a mixture of pain and wretchedness.

When Tommy's feet hit the foyer floor, he had the urge to let his legs crumble under him so he could kiss the black and white tiles. *If I drop, I'll never get up.* Instead, he chuckled with relief. What felt like a shard of glass moved in his throat. *It doesn't matter*, he told himself. He was on his way now and soon he'd be far away from Mable House.

His bedroom was directly to the left of the stairs. A few shuffling steps and he was in the tiny room. It seemed like months since he'd spent his first night in the narrow bed. He was pleased to see his pack was propped up next to his guitar on the floor. It seemed Lizzy had packed for him.

He bent to retrieve his belongings and toppled to the side, coming down on one knee with a jarring *thump*.

"Just for a minute." He spoke to the empty room and sank onto his butt.

He watched the light fading from orange to purple; it fell through the small window in a long, uneven rectangle. He'd wasted so much time chasing his dreams that he never stopped to wonder if he was happy. Nothing he'd done since leaving Adeline had come close to feeling like happiness. Yet even with his throat destroyed and the pain boiling his insides, he felt a sudden sense of contentment. A feeling that he was moving in the right direction.

Standing was much easier than he'd anticipated. His legs were stable and the sickness was settling. He made it through the house with little effort. Just as he'd hoped, the keys were on a hook near the back door. Barely breaking stride, he grabbed them and headed outside.

Why had he thought it was so late? The backyard was bathed in golden light. Sunshine dappled even the Hills Hoist into a magical glow. Tommy clamped his arm to his side, barely noticing the pain. With no sign of Lizzy or Soona, he made his way around the side of the building to where the Holden sat amongst the long grass.

The driver's door opened with a rusty croak. A faint odour filled the cab, a mixture of honey and lavender that sent a shiver of pleasure down his spine. He wondered what Lizzy had done to the vehicle to make it smell so appealing, but the thought was brief, fleeting. Taking a quick look over both shoulders, he inserted the key.

Please start. His lips moved without sound. The nauseated feeling together with the boiling agony in his stomach had eased, but the desire to escape remained.

Whatever was going on in Mable House, Tommy's gut told him it was time to make tracks.

He turned the key. The ancient engine rumbled to life with an immediacy belonging to a brand-new vehicle just off the assembly line. If his voice still worked, Tommy would have whooped out a cheer. Instead, he settled for a throaty chuckle. Lizzy lied about the Ute being out of action. He wondered what else she'd been deceitful about. His voice? His appendix? The idea that she'd lied about how sick he was should have made him angry, but as the Ute rolled away from the ramshackle hospital, all Tommy felt was relief.

The ride was smoother than he remembered, like coasting over newly laid marble. He checked the rearview mirror, half expecting Lizzy to be running behind the Ute waving her fist. Nothing but sunshine. He smiled and turned on the radio. A sweet melody filled the cab. Relaxing into the seat, he imagined Adeline's face when he returned home. She'd be upset at first, demanding an explanation. Her anger wouldn't last, it wasn't in her nature to be unkind – that's why he loved her so much.

Tommy didn't have any particular plan in mind beyond getting to the roadhouse. He'd park the Ute and let the universe sort the rest out for him. The road ahead was streaked with rivers of brilliant sunshine so bright, it took his breath away.

* * *

"Well, that's that, I suppose." Lizzy stood over Tommy's body, arms folded.

The young man lay sprawled on the floor as if he'd sat on the narrow bed and toppled forward. His right hand still held the handle of his guitar bag, fingers curled as if even in death he couldn't let it go. Somehow he'd made it down the stairs and into the small bedroom, but the infection in his abdomen had been too widespread. All the movement probably hastened his death.

"Sunshine?" Soona shuffled around near Tommy's head.

"Not anymore." Lizzy shook her head. "Where on earth did he think he was going?" She didn't expect Soona to answer. "We'll have to get rid of him. If the police come, they'll try to say it was my fault even though I did everything I could to help the man." Her voice rose slightly, taking on a wounded quality. "Another problem dumped in my lap. It's like when one of the patients had that accident and —"

Soona rocked on her toes and darted towards the door. Lizzy's hand shot out and grabbed the bigger woman by the collar of her shirt. "Hand it over." Lizzy gave the woman a shake. "You didn't think I knew, did you?"

Soona's brown eyes drifted away, fixing on something in the distance. She let out a series of shrieks, but when Lizzy twisted her collar, Soona plunged her grease-stained hand into her pocket and produced Tommy's phone.

"How many times have I told you not to take things that don't belong to you?" Lizzy snatched the phone and expertly opened the back, removing the battery. "I'll have to smash this." She waved the battery towards Tommy's lifeless body. "They can trace people with these things." She let out a long-tired breath. "Such a shame, a young man in his prime." She stared at the body in silence, a frown drawing her thick eyebrows together. "Oh well. Grab his shoulders, I'll take his legs. The sooner we bury him, the quicker you can get back to fixing the Ute."

If you enjoyed this book, please let others know by leaving a quick review on Amazon. Also, if you spot anything untoward in the paperback, get in touch. We strive for the best quality and appreciate reader feedback.

editor@thebookfolks.com

www.thebookfolks.com

Also by Anna Willett:

BACKWOODS RIPPER
RETRIBUTION RIDGE
UNWELCOME GUESTS
CRUELTY'S DAUGHTER
SMALL TOWN NIGHTMARE

Made in the USA
Lexington, KY
30 June 2019